6542 MAR 68

DOCTOR IN THE HOUSE

By the author of

DOCTOR AT SEA

THE CAPTAIN'S TABLE

DOCTOR AT LARGE

Doctor in the House

RICHARD GORDON

'A parcel of lazy, idle fellars, that are always smoking and drinking, and lounging . . . a parcel of young cutters and carvers of live people's bodies, that disgraces the lodgings.'

Bob Sawyer's landlady in PICKWICK PAPERS

London
MICHAEL JOSEPH

First published by
MICHAEL JOSEPH LTD
26 *Bloomsbury Street*
*London, W.C.*1
MARCH 1952
SECOND IMPRESSION MARCH 1952
THIRD IMPRESSION MARCH 1952
FOURTH IMPRESSION APRIL 1952
FIFTH IMPRESSION APRIL 1952
SIXTH IMPRESSION JUNE 1952
SEVENTH IMPRESSION JULY 1952
EIGHTH IMPRESSION JULY 1952
NINTH IMPRESSION SEPTEMBER 1952
TENTH IMPRESSION OCTOBER 1952
ELEVENTH IMPRESSION DECEMBER 1952
TWELFTH IMPRESSION FEBRUARY 1953
THIRTEENTH IMPRESSION MARCH 1953
FOURTEENTH IMPRESSION APRIL 1953
FIFTEENTH IMPRESSION JULY 1953
SIXTEENTH IMPRESSION SEPTEMBER 1953
SEVENTEENTH IMPRESSION OCTOBER 1953
EIGHTEENTH IMPRESSION (RE-SET) JANUARY 1954
NINETEENTH IMPRESSION MARCH 1954
TWENTIETH IMPRESSION APRIL 1954
TWENTY-FIRST IMPRESSION JUNE 1954
TWENTY-SECOND IMPRESSION JULY 1954
TWENTY-THIRD IMPRESSION JULY 1954
TWENTY-FOURTH IMPRESSION SEPTEMBER 1954
TWENTY-FIFTH IMPRESSION FEBRUARY 1955
TWENTY-SIXTH IMPRESSION APRIL 1955
TWENTY-SEVENTH IMPRESSION SEPTEMBER 1955
TWENTY-EIGHTH IMPRESSION OCTOBER 1955
TWENTY-NINTH IMPRESSION DECEMBER 1955
THIRTIETH IMPRESSION FEBRUARY 1956
THIRTY-FIRST IMPRESSION (RE-SET) OCTOBER 1956
THIRTY-SECOND IMPRESSION MARCH 1957
THIRTY-THIRD IMPRESSION MAY 1957
THIRTY-FOURTH IMPRESSION NOVEMBER 1957
THIRTY-FIFTH IMPRESSION SEPTEMBER 1958

Set and printed in Great Britain by Tonbridge Printers Ltd, Peach Hall Works, Tonbridge, Kent, in Baskerville eleven point two point leaded, on paper made by Henry Bruce at Currie, Midlothian, and bound by James Burn at Esher, Surrey

To
JO

NOTE

St. Swithin's Hospital does
not exist; neither do its staff,
students, nor patients.

1

THE large and completely unused set of surgical
instruments that my father kept in his consulting-
room held for the old gentleman the melancholy
fascination of a hopefully gathered layette to an ageing
childless wife. For twenty years he had not troubled to
exercise the self-deception that he might one day come
to use them. They lay in the slots of their metal trays,
fitting in with each other like the pieces of a Chinese
puzzle. There was a sharp-toothed circular trephine for
boring holes in the skull; bone forceps like a pair of
shiny pliers; a broad hacksaw for amputations; scissors
with long, sharp blades; probes, trocars, and bistouries;
and a row of scalpels as impotent as a line of ceremonial
swords.

The instruments were in a heavy black wooden box
with his name in copperplate script on its tarnished
metal label. He had stowed it away some years ago at
the bottom of a tall cupboard in the corner, where it had
become silted over with old medical journals, out-of-
date diaries, and bright advertisements from the big
drug firms that he had slung in there from time to time
with the vague belief that he might want to refer to
them one day. Occasionally, rummaging his way through
the dusty papers, he would uncover the box and light up
in himself a momentary glow of frustration: he had once

been convinced he was going to be a great surgeon, and the instruments were an expensive gift from his admiring mother the day he qualified as a doctor.

My grandparents were, unhappily, the only ones to share his confidence in his professional destination. The first step in becoming a surgeon of even mediocre ability is the acquisition of the Fellowship of the Royal College, an examination he sat regularly twice a year for six years before he faced up to the truth that his ability was not a powerful enough propellant for his ambition. His history after that was the not disagreeable one of a good many other unsuccessful young surgeons: he married and went into general practice in the provinces.

When he saw the brass plate being screwed on to his new doorpost he recognized it as the coffin-lid of his surgical aspirations. For a few months he was bitter at his abandonment of specialization, but his resentment was rapidly smoothed down by the heavy planes of domesticity, busy practice, and the momentous trivia of provincial social life. He became a prosperous, and even fairly efficient, general practitioner, and reflected on his dead ambitions only when he came across his case of instruments or thought seriously about the education of his son.

Like most doctors' children, I had from my earliest schooldays come to look upon a medical qualification like a hereditary title. Graduation seemed a future occurrence over which I had no control; indeed, neither my parents nor myself contemplated my earning a living by any other means. My father sometimes wondered timidly if I might fulfil his own surgical hopes, but experience had made him guarded in predicting his son's postgraduate attainments. I had certainly not demonstrated in adolescence any aptitude for my already settled career. Up to the age of six I had a habit of pulling to pieces birds and small mammals ingeniously trapped in the garden, and this was thought by my parents indicative of a natural inclination towards the biological sciences. The practice of medicine was to me no more than a succession of mysterious people coming twice a day through the front door, and the faint tang of antiseptic which had been in my nostrils as long as I could remember, like the scent of the sea to a fisherman's son.

Once my father stood me up on his leather examination couch, on which the most respected bodies in the district had lain in their forbidding nakedness, and showed me the framed photograph that hung above it. It was the rugby team at his old hospital, the year he had managed to scrape into the side owing to a fortunate attack of diphtheria in the regular wing threequarter.

'Which one's you, daddy?' I asked, running my forefinger along the double row of solemn young men in shorts.

He indicated a thin fellow at the end of the back row.

'Good old St. Swithin's!' he muttered sadly. 'You'll be there one day, my lad. And mind you get in the first fifteen like your father did.'

His love for his old hospital, like one's affection for the youthful homestead, increased steadily with the length of time he had been shot of it. As a medical student, he had felt a surge of allegiance to the place only for an hour or so a week on the football field; now it represented a glowing period in his life when he was single, irresponsible, and bouncing with ambition. I grew into the impression that St. Swithin's combined the medical efficiency of the Mayo Clinic with the teaching of Hippocrates and the recreational facilities of the Wembley Stadium. For most of my schooldays the place was an ill-defined but agreeable and definite destination, like Heaven, and it was not until I found myself on the point of going there that I troubled to crystallize my thoughts about it.

St. Swithin's was, in fact, an undistinguished general hospital which spread its grey, insanitary-looking walls across a grimy section of North London. It was not even one of the oldest hospitals in the Metropolis, and as age is esteemed in England as the first of the virtues, this alone imbued the staff and students with a faint sense of inferiority. St. Swithin's did not possess the proud antiquity of St. Bartholomew's, which for several centuries looked on to the crisp green of Smithfield and the sweet waters of the Fleet tumbling unconfinedly into the Thames; nor was it as ancient as St. Thomas's over the River, which was already old when Shakespeare came to the Globe. Its origins were obscure, but there was a tradition that it was founded to deal with the outbreak of syphilis that rolled over Europe after the discovery of America, whence it had been imported by Columbus's sailors (so setting a persistent maritime habit). St. Swithin's had, however, been in existence sufficiently long for Londoners to accept it as one of the settled institutions of their city that seemed completely reliable, like Westminster Bridge or St. Paul's. It now attended only to the pale inhabitants of the streets crammed against its walls, to whom it had been for three or four generations simply 'The Hospital,' a place you went into and either got better or died according to your luck.

I had not seen St. Swithin's until the morning I was interviewed by the Dean of the Medical School. The Dean had replied to my father's explanatory letter with the assurance that the school was always glad to see the sons of former Swithin's men, but he added that he was nevertheless obliged by the Governors to inspect each candidate and allot places solely on the strength of the aptitude they showed for the practice of medicine. As the course of study was fixed by law for a time not less than six years, this struck me as a task comparable in difficulty with determining the sex of day-old chicks. For a week I was coached earnestly by my father on every question the Dean could possibly ask; then I put on my best suit and went up to London.

St. Swithin's was heavily disappointing. It was like the time I was taken to the Zoo to see my first elephant: it was distinctive enough, but not nearly so large, clean, and dignified as I had imagined.

I walked gingerly inside the forecourt, which was separated from the main road by a long line of heavy iron railings and a gatehouse. The court contained a few plane trees and a patch of pale grass in the centre, and a pair of large black statues representing St. Swithin's most renowned sons. On the right of the gate as you went in was Lord Larrymore, the famous Victorian physician who maintained for some years that he had almost discovered the cause of tuberculosis but was cruelly forestalled by Robert Koch in Germany. On the left you saw Sir Benjamin Bone, Larrymore's celebrated surgical contemporary, who was nearly appointed to the Queen's household but was dropped at the last minute because Her Majesty objected to the expensive, but distracting, aroma of cigars and brandy exuded all day from his person.

When St. Swithin's began to find its feet as a teaching hospital at the beginning of the century the staff were as aware of their lack of presentable antecedents as a newly rich family. These two gentlemen had therefore undergone a process of medical canonization and were invested with professional abilities and intellectual qualities certainly not indicated by their true histories. Shortly after they had been elected to the staff a quarrel broke out between them, and for thirty years afterwards they refused to speak to each other. Communication was necessary on professional matters, and this was conducted by short notes in the third person carried from one to the other by a hospital porter specially employed for the purpose. In the later part of his life Sir Benjamin refused to utter the name of his colleague at all, and gave no indication that he was conscious of the other's existence until he saw one New Year's Day that Larrymore had been given a barony and immediately died of apoplexy.

The two doctors now stared in placid, set annoyance at each other across the court, and were disturbed only by an occasional painting-up from the students and the indiscriminate droppings of the London pigeons. What they originally quarrelled about had long ago been forgotten, but it was probably too trivial to be of interest.

My attention wandered from replicas of St. Swithin's staff to their living counterparts. The personnel of the hospital seemed to be in a state of constant transition across the courtyard. The consultant physicians and surgeons could easily be picked out, for they always moved from one spot to another in public as if they were in a desperate hurry. This gave the impression that their services were urgently needed in many places at once, and was good for their professional reputations. The junior practitioners had quickly picked up the habit from their superiors. The housemen strode importantly across the courtyard, their short white coats flying behind them, their stethoscopes trailing from their necks, wearing the look of grave preoccupation seen only in the faces of very fresh doctors. This drab, hurrying band of physicians was sprinkled with nurses in long mauve dresses and starched white caps that turned up at the back like the tails of white doves. They tripped smartly from one block to another and to the Nurses' Home in the rear. Of the people in the court they were the only ones genuinely in a hurry, for they had so little time to themselves they devoured their lives with a perpetual rush to get on and go off duty.

The bulk of the pedestrians in the courtyard was made up of almost equally important-looking and hasty people whom I was unable to identify. Apart from the doctors and nurses, a hospital has to employ men and women from a good many other occupations to run it. There must be chefs to prepare the food and dieticians to tell them what to cook; girls to work the X-ray machines and wardmaids to scrub the floors; physiotherapists to prevent the patients' muscles melting away in bed, and occupational therapists to stop their minds being similarly affected by showing them how to make mats, rugs, stuffed horses, and other unexciting articles while they are imprisoned in the wards. There must be liftmen and laundrymaids, porters and padres, stokers and statisticians; and as all these people must be paid and controlled there has to be a large number of clerks, typists, and secretaries to do so. The staff at St. Swithin's had come to outnumber the patients by four to one and now seemed to be expanding naturally, like a water-lily covering a small pond.

There were patients, too, in the courtyard. A couple of them lay on each side of the statues in their beds,

tucked up firmly in red blankets and sucking con-
valescence from the dirty London air. A few more
hobbled about on their sticks, tossed helplessly in the
strong cross-currents of hospital activity; one or two
fortunate ones had found quiet alcoves and stayed there,
like trout backing under the bank of a rocky stream.
And, as I watched, there passed through the whole lot
a cheery-looking man jauntily propelling a six-foot
barrow with a stiff canvas cover towards a small door
in one corner labelled 'Mortuary.'

I asked for the office of the Dean, Dr. Lionel Loftus,
F.R.C.P. A porter showed me into a small bare waiting-
room decorated only by framed black-and-white
pictures of past deans, which ran along the walls like
a row of dirty tiles. As there were no chairs I sat on the
edge of the dark polished table and swung my legs. The
surroundings, and a week of my father's coaching, had
made me depressed and nervous. My mind was filled
with the awkward questions that Dr. Loftus was even
then contemplating asking me, and I found to my
surprise I could give no satisfactory replies to any of
them. I wondered what I should say if he simply asked
me why I wanted to be a doctor. The answer was, I
suppose, that neither my parents nor myself had the
originality to think of anything else, but this didn't seem
a suggestion likely to help me into the medical school.

This disheartening introspection was interrupted by
the waiting-room door opening. An old man stood on
the threshold, looking at me silently. He wore a heavy
black jacket buttoned high in the chest, narrow trousers,
and a two-inch collar. In his hand he held a pair of
gold-rimmed pince-nez, which were attached to his
right lapel by a thick black silk ribbon. He was so thin,
so old, so pale, and so slow he could have taken his place

in the nearby post-mortem room without attracting attention.

He clipped his glasses on to his nose with a slow, shaky movement and inspected me more carefully. I leapt to my feet and faced him.

'Gordon?' croaked the old man from the doorway. 'Mr. Richard Gordon?'

'Yes, sir. That is correct, sir,' I replied with great respect.

'So you have come for entrance to St. Swithin's?' the old man asked slowly.

'Yes, sir, I have.'

He nodded, but without enthusiasm.

'Your father is a Swithin's man, I believe?'

'Oh yes, sir.'

'I am not the Dean,' he explained. 'I am the medical school Secretary. I was Secretary here long before you were born, my boy. Before your father, probably. I remember well enough when the Dean himself came up to be admitted.' He removed his glasses and pointed them at me. 'I've seen thousands of students pass through the school. Some of 'em have turned out good, and some of 'em bad—it's just like your own children.'

I nodded heartily, as I was anxious to please everyone.

'Now, young feller,' he went on more briskly, 'I've got some questions to ask you.'

I folded my hands submissively and braced myself mentally.

'Have you been to a public school?' he asked.

'Yes.'

'Do you play rugby football or association?'

'Rugby.'

'Do you think you can afford to pay the fees?'

'Yes.'

He grunted, and without a word withdrew. Left alone, I diverted my apprehensive mind by running my eye carefully over the line of black-and-white deans, studying each one in turn. After ten minutes or so the old man returned and led me in to see the living holder of the office.

Dr. Loftus was a short, fat, genial man with wispy white hair like pulled-out cotton wool. He was sitting at an old-fashioned roll-topped desk that was stacked untidily with folders, copies of medical journals, letters, and reference books. On top of these he had thrown a Homburg hat, a pair of yellow gloves, and his stethoscope. He was obviously in a hurry.

'Sorry to keep you waiting, old man,' he said cheerily, 'I was held up at a post-mortem. Have a seat.'

I sat down on a hard leather chair beside the desk.

'Now,' the Dean began. 'Have you been to a public school?'

'Yes.'

'Your people can afford the fees and that sort of thing?'

'I believe so.'

'You play rugby, I suppose?'

'Yes, sir.'

The Dean began to look interested.

'What position?' he asked.

'Wing three-quarter.'

He drew a pad of paper towards him and pencilled fifteen dots on it in rugby formation.

'Threequarter . . .' he murmured to himself. 'How old are you?' he asked sharply.

'Almost eighteen, sir.'

'Umm. First fifteen at school?'

16

'Oh yes, sir.'

The Dean traced lines through his dots, crossed others out, and rustled through a sheaf of typewritten papers beside him. He jerked back in his chair and inspected me closely all over.

'You're rather thin, aren't you,' he announced. 'I suppose you've got the speed?'

'I've got cups for the hundred,' I told him eagerly.

'Well, you may shape well. Lucky you're a three. The hospital's full of forwards,' he added in disgust.

He frowned at his paper pad for a few seconds. His face suddenly lightened, and I saw he had come to a decision: my hands gripped the arms of the chair as I waited to receive it. Rising, he shook me briskly by the hand and told me he had pleasure in admitting me to St. Swithin's.

I wondered for some time afterwards how he had been able to discover from these questions that I had the attributes of a successful doctor, but I later found out that even this brief interview was superfluous, as the Dean always took the advice of his old secretary and told applicants this man disliked the look of that there were no vacancies.

2

THE medical school of St. Swithin's hospital was an offshoot of the main buildings and had its own entrance on the main road. It was a tall, gloomy structure that held three floors of laboratories, an anatomical dissection room, a lecture theatre that was clothed in perpetual dusk, and the smelliest lavatories in the district.

The school had been built by the richest brewer in London, who was happily knocked over by a hansom outside the hospital gates one slippery winter's morning in 1875. He was restored to health and normal locomotion in the wards, and to show his gratitude he purchased his peerage the following year by founding the school. The place was now far too old, dark, and small for the requirements of the students, but as the hospital could see little prospect of the accident being repeated it was impossible to tear it down.

At the beginning of October thirty new students collected there for a lecture of welcome and introduction by the Dean. Carrying a new and shiny loose-leaf folder under my arm, I walked up the stone steps for the first time and into the dingy, small entrance hall. The brewer's name was carved in stone over the doorway to indicate the hospital's enduring gratitude, and was reflected in green and gold across the face of the

King George public house opposite. Below his chiselled title were the serpents entwined round the winged staff, the doctors' universal trademark, and below that Hippocrates' discouraging aphorism 'The Art is Long.'

The hall, which was painted in yellow and green, contained a small kiosk bearing the word 'Enquiries' in which a porter had firmly shut himself by pulling down the glass window, turning his back on it, and reading the *Daily Mirror* with undistractable attention. There was a short row of clothes-hooks as heavy as an orchard in August, and a long notice board thickly covered by overlapping sheets of paper.

I glanced at the board as I passed, feeling some faint obligation to do so. The notices were an untidy jumble of typewritten official instructions about lectures, examinations, and so forth, and scraps of paper torn from notebooks scrawled with students' writing. These indicated the pathetic undercurrents of medical school life as much as the agony column of *The Times* reflects those below the existence of the middle class. The first to catch my eye was in green ink, and said angrily 'Will the *gentleman* (underlined four times heavily) who took my umbrella from the physiology lab last Thursday bring it back? How can I afford a new one?' Next to it was a faded invitation for two students to make up a party to dissect an abdomen in Edinburgh during the vacation, adding temptingly 'Digs and abdomen fixed up. Good pubs.' There were lists of text-books for sale, triumphantly set up by men who had passed their examinations and therefore had no necessity to learn anything else; several small earnest printed appeals for support of the local Student Christian Association; and a number of unfulfilled wants, from a disarticulated foot to a cheap motor-bike.

A hand on the wall pointed upwards 'To the Lecture Theatre.' The way was by a thin iron spiral staircase that ended in darkness. I mounted it, and found myself against a dull brown door attached to a spring that creaked violently as it opened.

The door led to the back of a steep tier of narrow wooden benches rising from the lecturer's desk like a football stand. Behind the desk were three large blackboards screwed to the walls, which were otherwise panelled with stained perpendicular planks. The roof was lost in a criss-cross of thin iron girders through which half a dozen electric globes were suspended to supplement the thin light that filtered through the windows under the eaves.

I sat down shyly at the extreme end of the last row of benches. Most of the new students had already arrived, and had scattered themselves here and there in the tier of seats. A few seemed to know one another and were conversing softly among themselves. The rest were isolated and silent and looked blankly at the blackboards ahead of them, like a congregation in church waiting for the service.

We were as variegated as a bunch of conscripts. Most of the students were my own age, but in the row immediately below me a middle-aged bald-headed man was scribbling some private notes with a pencil in an exercise book; every now and then he jumped, looked round him anxiously, and fidgeted like a schoolgirl. The only other occupant of my row was a pale youth with untidy ginger hair who appeared to be about fifteen, and was reading *The Origin of Species* with alarming concentration.

The clock on the wall above the lecturer's desk reached twenty past ten: the Dean was late again. We later found that this was a common occurrence as he emphasized his complete superiority over the students in his appointments by being scrupulously unpunctual. I was still staring expectantly at the blackboards when the door behind me groaned and another student entered.

'I say, do you mind if I squeeze in?' the newcomer asked. 'I hate being far from the exit.'

I shifted along the hard bench hastily. The new man seemed so much at ease in his surroundings it appeared he was senior to the rest of the waiting class. He was certainly more distinctive in his appearance. He was a tall, good-looking young man with thick black hair and a small moustache. He wore a long brown hacking jacket, narrow corduroy trousers, a green shirt, and a yellow silk square instead of a tie. He set down on the floor beside him a polished black walking-stick, and taking a monocle from his breast pocket surveyed his companions through it with blatant disgust.

'Good God,' he said.

He then opened a copy of *The Times* and began reading it.

The abashed silence in the room was maintained for another ten minutes, broken only by my new neighbour noisily turning over the pages. At ten thirty, half an hour late, a small door behind the desk opened and the Dean bounced in. He was all smiles and geniality. He stood for a moment and beamed at the class like a bishop inspecting his confirmation candidates.

The Dean was not only late but in a tearing hurry. He briefly welcomed us to St. Swithin's, made a few remarks about its history and traditions, rapidly ran through the ethics of the medical profession, and explained that in future we would be bound by professional secrecy, and forbidden to make love to our patients' wives, do abortions, or walk on the grass in the hospital courtyard. He flung a few final remarks of encouragement at his listeners and shot off. His address had lasted seventeen minutes, and the only acknowledgment that the student next to me had made of his presence was folding his paper twice over and reading it under cover of the man in front.

'Oh, he's finished, has he?' said the man with the paper, as the scuffling of students getting to their feet disturbed him. He peered at the clock through his monocle. 'H'm,' he remarked. 'He's cut three minutes off his best time so far. Did he leave out that bit about the hospital traditions?'

'No,' I told him. 'He seemed to have quite a lot to say about them.'

The student raised his free eyebrow. 'Did he now? Then he's speeding up his delivery. Next year I bet the old boy gets it down to fifteen minutes dead.'

I was very afraid of this superior and critical young man, but I could not help asking a question.

'You've heard the lecture before?' I said hesitantly. 'I mean, you haven't just arrived in the hospital like the rest of us?'

'This makes the fourth time I've heard old Lofty say his little piece,' he replied, smiling faintly. 'Wouldn't have come to-day, except that I got the dates mixed. I was expecting an anatomy lecture.'

The rest of the class was filing past us through the door and clattering down the iron stairs. We rose and joined the end of the line.

'You must be a very senior student,' I said respectfully.

'Not a bit of it, old boy.' My companion absently

flicked a crumpled piece of paper to one side with his stick. 'I'm not a minute senior to you and the end of the year will probably find me back here again.'

'But surely,' I said from behind him as we descended the stairs, 'if you have four years' study to your credit . . .'

He laughed.

'Ah, the ingenuousness of youth! Four years' study, or at least four years' spasmodic attendance at the medical school, is of no significance. Exams, my dear old boy, exams,' he explained forcibly. 'You'll find they control your progress through hospital like the signals on a railway line—you can't go on to the next section if they're against you. I've come down in my anatomy four times now,' he added cheerfully.

I condoled with him over this quadruple misfortune.

'Don't sympathize, old boy. I appreciate it, but it's wasted. All my failures were achieved with careful forethought. As a matter of fact, it's much more difficult to fail an examination skilfully than to pass the damn thing. To give that impression of once again just having been unfortunate in the choice of the questions, you know. . . . Come along and have a beer. The King George will be open.'

We crossed the road and the experienced examinee thrust open the door of the saloon bar with his cane. I had meanwhile decided the medical course was a far more complicated affair than I had imagined.

The King George was one of those dark, cosy, pokey little pubs that, like brewers' drays and paralytic drunks, seem to be disappearing from the London drinking scene. The small saloon bar was heavy with dark wood and thick mirrors splashed with gilt *fleurs de lis*. The dingy white ceiling was gathered into plaster rosettes, the lamps sprouted out of the walls on curly metal stems, and in the corner a pale palm drooped over a large brass pot.

The influence of the hospital on the King George was noticeable immediately. Between the mirrors the walls were covered with framed photographs of past rugby and cricket teams, from which there stared down defiantly several hundred young gentlemen who were now respectable and ageing practitioners all over the country. Above the bar, in a glass case like a stuffed pike, was the rugby ball with which the fifteen had once won the hospitals' cup for the third year running. Next to it there hung a large, old-fashioned brass fireman's helmet. Behind the beer taps a fat old man in an apron, waistcoat, and grey trilby hat stared gloomily across the empty bar.

'Good morning, Padre,' my guide called cheerily.

The old man gave a smile of welcome and stretched his hand over the counter.

'Good morning, sir!' he exclaimed. 'Well! This is a treat to see you here again! Back for the new session is it, sir?'

'Every autumn, Padre, I return faithfully to my studies. Allow me to introduce a new student—what's your name, old boy?'

'Gordon—Richard Gordon.'

'Mr. Gordon, Padre. My name's Grimsdyke, by the way,' he explained.

The landlord shook hands heartily.

'And very pleased to meet you, sir!' he said warmly. 'I expect we'll be seeing some more of you in the next five or six years, eh? What's it to be, gentlemen?'

'Bitter for me,' said Grimsdyke, settling himself on a wooden stool. 'Will you take the same?'

I nodded.

'I should explain,' Grimsdyke continued, as the land-lord filled the glasses, 'that this gentleman behind the bar is really called Albert something or other, I believe. . . .'

'Mullins, sir.'

'Mullins, yes. But no one in Swithin's would have the faintest idea who you were talking about. For the memory of living man he has been known as the Padre . . . how many years have you been dishing out the booze here, Padre?'

'Thirty-five, sir, just on.'

'There you are! He remembers the present senior physicians when they were students themselves—and a pretty rowdy crowd, by all accounts. There was the incident of Loftus introducing a carthorse into the Matron's bedroom . . .'

The Padre chuckled loudly.

'That was a real night, sir! Nothing like it happens any more, worse luck.'

'Well look at the beer you sell now,' said Grimsdyke reproachfully. 'Anyhow,' he went on to me, 'this pub is now as indispensable a part of the hospital as the main operating theatre.'

'But why the Padre?' I asked cautiously.

'Oh, it's a custom started by the housemen. One can say in front of patients "I'm popping out to Chapel at six this evening" without causing alarm, whereas a poor view might be taken by the old dears if they got the idea their doctors drank. Besides, the old boy has a not un-clerical function. He's a sort of father confessor, Dutch uncle, and Dr. Barnardo to the boys sometimes— you'll find out about it before you've been here much longer.'

25

I nodded acknowledgment for the information. For a minute we drank our beer in silence.

'There's just another thing,' I began.

'Speak on, my dear old boy. I am always too glad to give what help I can to new students. After all, I have been one myself now five times.'

I pointed silently at the shiny brass helmet.

'Ah, yes, the sacred helm of St. Swithin's by God! Feared and coveted in every medical school in London. You must learn about that before you go any further. How it got there, no one knows. It's been the property of the rugger club for longer than even the Padre can remember, so I suppose one of the boys must have lifted it on a Saturday night years ago. Anyway, it has now become a totem, a fetish, a fiery cross. For the big matches against Guy's or Mary's and so on the helmet is laid on the touchline for luck and inspiration. Afterwards it is filled with beer and emptied by all members of the team in turn.'

'It would hold a lot of beer,' I observed nervously.

'It does. However, on the occasion of qualification, engagement, birthday, marriage, or death of rich relatives, the thing is taken down and the man stood a helmet of beer by his friends. Are you engaged or married?' he asked suddenly.

'Good Lord, no!' I said. I was shocked. 'I've only just left school.'

'Well . . . anyhow, it's quite a point with me at the moment. But to return to our helmet. Often the gentlemen of lesser institutions attempt to steal it—we had quite a tussle with a gang of roughs from Bart's last season. Once last year some fellows from Tommy's got it as far as the River, but we won it back from them on Westminster Bridge. By Jove, that was an evening!' He smiled at the memory. 'One of the chaps got a fractured mandible. Will you have another beer?'

I shook my head.

'No thanks. I don't drink much, you know. Hardly at all, in fact. Only if I've been out for a long walk or something and I'm thirsty.'

I saw Grimsdyke wince.

'Of course, one must remember . . .' he began. 'You will find that in a little while at St. Swithin's you will learn enough bad habits to make life bearable. However, there is time enough for that. Padre,' he called. 'The other half for me, if you please.'

'Could you tell me . . .?' I began, feeling I had better collect all the information I could from my companion while he was talkative.

'Yes?'

'Why—why do you fail your examinations on purpose?'

Grimsdyke looked inscrutable.

'That is a little secret of my own,' he said darkly. 'Maybe I'll let you into it one day, old boy.'

I learnt about Grimsdyke's little secret earlier than he expected. It was common knowledge in the medical school and seeped down into the first-year students within a few weeks of their arrival.

Grimsdyke's reluctance to pass examinations was wholly the fault of his grandmother, a well-to-do old lady who had passed the long-drawn-out twilight of her life in Bournemouth. As she had nothing else to occupy her she developed a wide selection of complaints, which were soothed away, all in good time, by the expensive attentions of her charming physicians. Her regard for the medical profession mounted with each indisposition, and was tempered only with the regret that she had not a single medical gentleman in her own family. The only person who could have rectified the omission was young Grimsdyke, and she conceived the idea while he was still at school of enticing him into the profession by offering to pay his expenses for the course. Unfortunately, the grandmother shortly afterwards developed a malady beyond the abilities of her doctors and was carried away; but her will contained a clause bequeathing a thousand a year to the young man during the time that he was a medical student.

Grimsdyke did not immediately realize the full significance of this, and had begun his first year's study at St. Swithin's before it dawned on him that he had an excellent opportunity to spend the rest of his life in London on a comfortable allowance without the tedium of doing any work. He therefore took great pains always to fail his examinations. He came to the hospital once or twice a week, paid his fees promptly, and behaved himself, which was sufficient for St. Swithin's. He had a flat in Knightsbridge, an old two-seater car (known as The Ulcer, because it was always breaking down), a large number of friends, and plenty of spare time. 'I sometimes think,' he would admit to his cronies, 'I have discovered the secret of graceful living.'

About the time that I joined the medical school Grimsdyke's spacious days became limited. He had fallen in love with a girl and proposed to her, but she was a shrewd young woman and not only discovered the secret of his existence but refused to accept him unless he altered it.

'An embryo doctor, yes,' Grimsdyke would explain sadly, 'but a chronic hanger-on in a medical school, no. I was obliged to go out and buy some books. The power of women, my dear old boy. It is for them that men climb mountains, fight wars, go to work, and such unpleasant things.'

She must have had the personality of a Barbary slave-master, for he thenceforward applied himself to his studies as enthusiastically as anyone else in the hospital.

3

As there were no classes arranged for the day of the Dean's lecture I had the afternoon to myself. I slipped off quietly from the King George shortly after a bunch of senior students burst in and started a noisy drinking session with Grimsdyke. The light-hearted way which my new companions slipped down pints of beer alarmed me. I drank very little, for I had recently left school and was under the impression that more than two glasses of beer ruined your rugger and led to equally serious moral degeneration.

'So you are going in for—um—medicine?' my house-master had said to me during my final term.

'Yes, sir.'

'A very—er—esteemed profession, Gordon, as you should know. Unfortunately, I find the means of entry to it seems to have a bad influence on boys of even the highest character. No doubt the effect of dealing daily with the—um—fundamental things in life, as it were, is some excuse. Yet I must warn you to exercise continual restraint.'

'Oh yes, sir. I will, of course, sir.'

'I expect you will soon become as bad as the rest,' he sighed. His small opinion of medical students sprang largely from the days when he had been reading theology at Cambridge and, on his attempt to break up a noisy party of medicals in the adjoining rooms late one night, he had been forcibly administered an enema of Guinness's stout.

I had lunch alone at the A.B.C. and went down to a medical bookshop in Bloomsbury to buy some text-books. I had to get a copy of Gray's *Anatomy*, the medical student's bible, an unquestionable authority on anatomy as Hansard on a parliamentary debate. When I saw the book my heart sank under its weight. I flicked over the two thousand foolscap pages of detailed anatomical description split up by beautiful bold drawings of yellow nerves, bright red arteries, and blue veins twining their way between dissected brown muscles that opened like the petals of an unfolding flower. I wondered how any-one could ever come to learn all the tiny facts packed between its covers as thickly as the grains in a sack of wheat. I also bought a set of volumes giving directions for dissection of the body, a thick tome on physiology full of graphs and pictures of vivisected rabbits, and a book of Sir William Osler's addresses to medical students.

'Is there anything else, sir?' the assistant asked politely.

'Yes,' I said. 'A skeleton. Do you happen to have a skeleton?'

'I'm sorry, sir, but we're out of skeletons at the moment. The demand on them is particularly heavy at this time of the year.'

I spent the rest of the afternoon hunting a skeleton for use in the evenings with the anatomical text-books. I found one in a shop off Wigmore Street and took it back to my digs. Most landladies had become accustomed to a skull to be dusted on the mantelpiece and a jumble of dried bones in the corner, but students moving into lodgings that had previously sheltered such inoffensive young men as law or divinity pupils were sometimes turned out on the grounds that their equipment precipitated in the good lady a daily attack of the creeps.

*   *   *   *   *

For the first two years of their course medical students are not allowed within striking distance of a living patient. They learn the fundamentals of their art harmlessly on dead ones. The morning after the Dean's lecture the new class was ordered to gather in the anatomical dissecting room to begin the term's work.

The dissecting room was a high, narrow apartment on the ground floor of the medical school that exhaled a strong smell of phenol and formaldehyde. A row of tall frosted glass windows filled one wall, and the fluorescent lights that hung in strips from the ceiling gave the students themselves a dead, cyanotic look. The wall opposite the windows supported a length of blackboard covered with drawings of anatomical details in coloured chalks. In one corner was a stand of pickled specimens, like the bottles on a grocer's shelves, and in the other a pair of assembled skeletons grinned at each other, suspended from gallows like the minatory remains of highwaymen. Down the room were a dozen high, narrow, glass-topped tables in two rows. And on the tables, in different stages of separation, were six or seven dissected men and women.

I looked at the bodies for the first time curiously. They were more like mummies than recently dead humans. All were the corpses of old people, and the preserving process to which they had been subjected had wrinkled them beyond that of ageing. Four un-

32

touched subjects lay naked and ready for the new class, but at the other tables the senior students were already at work. Some of the groups had advanced so far that the part they were dissecting was unidentifiable to an unknowing onlooker like myself; and here and there a withered, contracted hand stuck out in silent supplication from a tight group of busy dissectors.

We stood nervously just inside the door waiting for instructions from the Professor of Anatomy. Each of us wore a newly starched white coat and carried a little canvas roll containing a pair of forceps, a freshly sharpened scalpel, and a small wire probe stuck into a pen-handle. The others, to impress their superiority on the newcomers, disregarded us completely.

The Professor had the reputation of an academic Captain Bligh. He was one of the country's most learned anatomists, and his views on the evolution of the hyoid bone in the throat were quoted to medical students in dissecting rooms from San Francisco to Sydney. His learned distinction was unappreciated by his students, however, all of whom were terrified of him.

He had several little unnerving peculiarities. For some reason the sight of a student walking into the medical school with his hands in his pockets enraged him. His private room was next to the main entrance, so it was convenient for him to shoot out and seize by the shoulders any man he saw through the window sauntering into the building in this way. He would shake him and abuse him thoroughly for some minutes before stepping back into his room to watch for the next one. This habit was thought unpleasant by the students, but nothing could be done about it because the Professor, who controlled the examinations, held the power of justice at all levels in the anatomy school.

The Professor appeared suddenly in the dissecting room through his private entrance. The hum of conversation at the tables immediately ceased and was replaced by serious, silent, activity.

He stood for some moments looking at his new class narrowly. The sight apparently did not please him. He grunted, and drawing a sheet of paper from the pocket of his white coat called a roll of our names in a voice rough with disgust. He was a tall thin man, shaped like a bullet. His bald head rose to a pointed crown and his body sloped outwards gently to his tiny feet far below. He wore a mangy ginger beard.

He put the list of names back in his pocket.

'Now listen to me, you fellows,' he began sternly. 'You've got to *work* in this department, d'you understand? I'm not going to put up with any slacking for a moment. Anatomy's tough—you can't learn it unless you put your backs into it. Any laziness here, and . . .' He jerked his thumb over his shoulder. 'Out! See?'

We nodded nervously, like a squad of recruits listening to their first drill sergeant.

'And I don't want to see any of you men slopping round with your hands in your pockets. It's all right for errand boys and pimps, but you're supposed to be medical students. The attitude is not only unanatomical but gives you osteoarthritis of the shoulder girdle in your middle age. No wonder you all grow up into a hunchbacked crowd of deformities! I know I'm ugly, but I can stand up straight, which is more than some of you people. Do you follow me?'

We assented briskly.

'Right. Well, get on with some work. The list

of parts for dissection is up on the board at the end there.'

With a final glare he disappeared through his door.

I had been allotted a leg for my first term's work. We dissected in pairs, two men to each part. My partner was a student called Benskin—a large, sandy-haired man who wore under his white coat a green check shirt and a red tie with little yellow dogs on it.

'What ho,' said Benskin.

'Good morning,' I replied politely.

'Are you conversant with the mysteries of anatomical dissection?' he asked.

'No. Not at all.'

'Nor I.'

We looked at each other silently for a few seconds.

'Perhaps we had better read the instructions in the dissecting manual,' I suggested.

We sat down on a pair of high wooden stools and propped the book against the dead thigh on the table in front of us. After turning over several preliminary pages we reached a drawing of a plump leg with bold red lines over it.

'That seems to be our skin incision,' I said, pointing to one of the lines. 'Will you start, or shall I?'

Benskin waved a large hand generously.

'Go ahead,' he said.

I drew a breath, and lightly touched the greasy rough skin. With my new scalpel I made a long sweeping incision.

'I think I've cut the wrong thing,' I said, glancing at the book.

'It doesn't look quite like the picture,' Benskin admitted. 'Perhaps we ought to raise some help.'

There were a pair of demonstrators in the dissecting

room—young doctors passing grey years in the anatomy department for small wages in the hope of being appointed to the surgical staff of St. Swithin's in middle age. They flitted from one group of students to another like bees in a herbaceous border, pollinating each pair with knowledge. Both of them were far away from our table.

At that moment I caught sight of Grimsdyke, in a shining starched coat, strolling between the dissectors like an Englishman in a Suez bazaar. He waved languidly to me.

'How are you progressing?' he asked, crossing to our table. 'Good God, is that as far as you've got?'

'It's very difficult,' I explained. 'You see, we don't quite know how to start. Could you give us a bit of a hand?'

'But certainly, my dear old boy,' Grimsdyke said, picking up a scalpel. 'I have now dissected four legs and consider I have something of a flair for the knife. This is the gluteus maximus muscle.'

Grimsdyke slit his way rapidly through the muscles and in half an hour did our work for the week.

*　　*　　*　　*　　*

The routine of lectures and dissection passed the time agreeably. After a few weeks I began to distinguish more sharply the personalities of my fellow students, as an eye gradually sees the objects in a darkened room. My dissecting partner, Tony Benskin, was a cheery young man whose mental horizon was bounded by rugby football and beer drinking and clouded over only with a chronic scarcity of cash. Dissecting the fellow to our leg was the ginger-haired youth I had noticed at the Dean's lecture reading Darwin. He turned out to

be a quiet and disturbingly brilliant Welshman called
Evans, who started the course under the impetus of a
senior scholarship. Evans dissected away conscientiously
and efficiently from the start—which was fortunate, as
his own companion rarely put in an appearance in the
anatomy room at all. He was a handsome fellow named
John Bottle, whose interests in life were ballroom
dancing and the dogs. He spent most of his afternoons
in the palais and his evenings at Harringay or the White
City. The middle-aged man with the notebook I soon
discovered to be an ex-bank clerk called Sprogget, who
was left a little money after twenty years' looking at a
ledger and immediately fulfilled an almost forgotten
ambition of taking up medicine. Sprogget was unfortunate in being partnered by the most objectionable
student in the class—a man named Harris, whom
Grimsdyke named immediately the Keen Student.
Harris knew everything. His greased black hair,
parted precisely in the middle, and his thick-rimmed
spectacles popped frequently between a pair of
dissectors.

'You know, old man,' he would volunteer, 'you're
not doing that bit according to the book. You ought to
have exposed the nerve before you cut away the
tendons. Hope you don't mind my mentioning it, but
I thought it might save you a bit of trouble with the
Prof later. I say, you've made a mess of the brachial
artery, haven't you?'

He was incorrigible. He sat at the front of the
lectures and asked grave questions to which he already
knew the answers. He ate a lunch of sandwiches in
the locker room of the anatomy department, reading
a text-book; and his conversation was limited strictly
to anatomy. He regarded the barracking to which

he was inevitably subjected as another instance of persecution of the intellectuals.

Grimsdyke was a useful acquaintance, for his four years' start put him on familiar terms with the senior students. One afternoon shortly after my arrival he hailed me as I was walking out of the medical school doorway.

'I say, old lad,' he called. 'Come and meet Mike Kelly. He's secretary of the rugger club.'

There was a broad young man with a red face standing beside him. He wore an old tweed jacket with leather on the elbows and a brilliant yellow pullover.

'How do you do,' I said respectfully. Kelly was not only rugby secretary but two years senior to myself.

'Pleased to meet you,' said Kelly, crushing my hand. 'You play a bit, do you?'

'A bit. Threequarter.'

'Jolly good. The hospital's going to be short of good threes in a year or so. First fifteen at school, I take it?'

'Yes.'

'Which school?'

I told him.

'Oh,' said Kelly with disappointment. 'Well, there's no reason why they shouldn't turn out a decent player once in a while. We'll give you a run with the extra B fifteen on Saturday and see how you make out. Grimsdyke here's the captain. He'll fix you up.'

'The extra B is a bit of a joke,' Grimsdyke said as Kelly strode off. 'Actually, we are more of a social side than anything. Our boast is that we can take on any team at any game. Last summer we played a dance band at cricket, and I've arranged a shove-ha'penny match with the police for next month. I'll meet you here at lunchtime on Saturday and give you and that fat chap—what's his name . . .?'

'Benskin.'

'Benskin, that's right. I'll give you both a lift to the ground in my car. Don't worry about shirts and things.'

The St. Swithin's ground was in a North London suburb, and the extra B was the only one of the half-dozen teams run by the hospital that was playing at home that week-end. The game was not brilliant and St. Swithin's ended up with a narrow win.

'Well done,' said Grimsdyke, as I was changing. 'You and that Benskin fellow shaped pretty well. You must both be horribly healthy. With any luck you might make the third fifteen before the season's out.'

'Thank you very much.'

'Now get a move on. It's after five and we don't want to waste time.'

'What's the hurry?' I asked.

Grimsdyke looked at me with amazement.

'Why, they open at five-thirty! We'll just make the King George, if we step on it.'

'Thank you,' I said. 'But I think I ought to go back to my digs. . . .'

'On Saturday night! Good Lord, old boy, that's not done at all! Hurry up and put your trousers on.'

Afraid of social errors in this new way of living, I obeyed. We arrived outside the King George as the Padre was opening the doors. Both teams pushed into the small saloon bar while a line of glass tankards clinked temptingly on the counter. Everyone was in a good humour, pleasantly tired and bathed. We were laughing and joking and clapping each other on the shoulder.

'Here you are,' Grimsdyke said, pushing a pint into my hand. 'There'll be a five-bob kitty.'

I handed over two half-crowns, thinking it was a great deal to spend on beer in one evening.

'Drink up!' Grimsdyke said a few minutes later. 'I'm just getting another round.'

Not wishing to appear unusual, I emptied the glass. A fresh one was immediately put into my fingers, but I timidly held it untouched for a while.

'You're slow,' said Benskin jovially, bumping into me. 'There's bags more left in the kitty.'

I took a quick gulp. I suddenly made the discovery that beer tasted most agreeable. The men round me were downing it with impunity, so why shouldn't I? I swallowed a large draught with a flourish.

With the third pint a strange sensation swept over me. I felt terribly pleased with myself. Damn it! I thought. I can drink with the best of them! Someone started on the piano and Benskin began to sing. I didn't know any of the words, but I joined in the choruses with the rest.

'Your drink, Mr. Gordon,' said the Padre, handing me another tankard.

I downed the fourth glass eagerly. But I felt the party had become confused. The faces and lights blurred into one another and the voices inexplicably came some-times from far away, sometimes right in my ear. Snatches of song floated into my brain like weed on a sluggish sea.

'*Caviar comes from the virgin sturgeon,*' Benskin chanted.
   '*Virgin sturgeon, very fine fish.*
   Virgin sturgeon needs no urgin'
   That's why caviar's a very rare dish.'

I wedged myself against the bar for support. Someone next to me was telling a funny story to two men and their laughter sounded far off and eerie, like the three witches'.

> *'That pair of red plush breeches*
> *That pair of red plush breeches,*

came from the piano corner.

> *'That pair of red plush bre-e-e-ehes*
> *That kept John Thomas warm.'*

'Are you feeling all right?' a voice said in my ear.

I mumbled something.

'What's that, old man?'

'Bit sick,' I confessed briefly.

'Hold on a moment. I'll take you back to your digs. Where's he live, Benskin? Help me to get him in the car someone. Oh, and bring something along in case he vomits.'

*　　*　　*　　*　　*

The next morning Grimsdyke came round to my lodgings.

'How is it?' he asked cheerily.

'I feel awfully ill.'

'Simply a case of hangover vulgaris, old boy. I assure you the prognosis is excellent. Here's half a grain of codeine.'

'What happened to me?' I asked.

Grimsdyke grinned.

'Let's say you've been blooded,' he said.

4

EVEN medical students must have somewhere to
live. The problem of finding suitable accommodation is difficult because they are always
disinclined to spend on mere food and shelter money
that would do equally well for beer and tobacco. And
they are not, as a rule, popular lodgers. They always
sit up late, they come in drunk on Saturdays, and they
have queer things in bottles in their bedrooms. On the
other hand, there are a small number of landladies who
think it a privilege to entertain a prospective doctor
under their roof. The connection with the profession
raises their social standing in the street, and the young
gentlemen can always be consulted over the dinner
table on the strictly private illnesses to which landladies
seem distressingly liable.

I started off in lodgings in Finchley, which were
clean, fairly cheap, and comfortable. The landlady had
a daughter, a tall, blank-faced brunette of nineteen, an
usherette at the local Odeon. One evening after I had
been there about six weeks she tapped at my bedroom
door.

'Are you in bed?' she asked anxiously.

'No,' I called through the door. 'I'm studying. What
is it?'

'It's me foot,' she said. 'I think I've sprained it or something. Will you have a look at it for me?'

'In the kitchen,' I replied guardedly. 'Take your stocking off and I'll be down in a minute.'

The following week she developed a pain in the calf, and the one after stiffness of the knee. When she knocked on the door and complained of a bad hip I gave notice.

I moved into a top-floor room of a lodging-house near Paddington Station. Its residents represented so many nationalities the directions for working its tricky and uncertain lavatories had to be set up in four different languages, as in the Continental expresses. There was another medical student there, a man from St. Mary's who kept tropical fish in a tank in his bedroom and practised Yogi.

As I had to take all my meals out I saw little of the other lodgers except when they passed on the stairs and said 'Excuse me' in bad English. In the room next to mine was a stout young blonde, but she lived very quietly and never disturbed anyone. One morning she was found strangled in Hyde Park, and after that I thought I ought to move again.

For the following twelve months I lived in a succession of boarding-houses. They were all the same. They had a curly hat-stand in the hall, a red stair-carpet worn grey in the middle, and a suspicious landlady. By the time I reached the end of the anatomy course I was tired of the smell of floor-polish, damp umbrellas, and frying; when I was offered a share in a flat in Bayswater I was so delighted I packed up and moved without even waiting to work out the week's rent.

The share was awarded to me through the good

offices of Tony Benskin, who lived there with four other students. There was John Bottle, the man who liked dancing and dogs; Mike Kelly, now Captain of the first fifteen; and a youth known about the hospital as Moronic Maurice, who had surprised the teaching staff and himself by finally passing his qualifying exams, and had gone off to practise the art, to the publicly expressed horror of the Dean, as house-surgeon to a small hospital in the country.

These four were really sub-tenants. The flat was leased by a final-year student, a pleasant fellow called Archie Broome, who had lived there during most of his time at St. Swithin's and took his friends as lodgers to help out with the rent.

'We're pretty free and easy there,' he explained to me in the King George. 'I hope you're not terribly particular about the time you have your meals or go to bed and that sort of thing?'

As I had found unpunctuality for meals was taken by landladies as a personal outrage and sitting up to midnight regarded as sinful, I told my prospective landlord warmly I didn't give a damn for such formalities.

'That's good,' Archie said. 'We usually kick in together for the groceries and beer and so forth, if that's all right with you. Here's the key, and you can move in when you like.'

I shifted the following afternoon. The flat was in a large, old, grimy block just by the Park, up a dark flight of stairs. I dropped my suitcases on the landing outside the door and fumbled for the key. While I was doing so the door opened.

Standing in the hallway was one of the most beautiful women I had ever seen. She was a tall blonde with a figure like a model in a dress-shop window. She wore slacks and a sweater, which sharply defined her slight curves. Taking her cigarette out with a long graceful hand, she said with great friendliness, 'Hello, Richard. Come on in and make yourself at home.'

'I'm afraid . . .' I began. 'I mean, I was looking for a fellow called Broome, you know. . . .'

'That's right,' she said. She had a slight, attractive, and unplaceable accent. 'The boys are all at the hospital at the moment, but just come in anyway. Would you like a cup of tea? My name's Vera.'

'How do you do,' I said politely. I picked up my cases and entered hesitantly. After conditioning myself to living with four coarse men being greeted by a delicate girl was puzzling.

'This is the sitting-room,' Vera continued. 'How about the tea?'

'No thanks. Very kind of you, but I've had some.'

'That's good, because I've got to go and change anyway. If you do want anything the kitchen's through there. Just look round as you please.'

The girl slipped through a door leading off the hall, leaving me in the centre of the sitting-room feeling like a participant in the opening scene of a bedroom farce. I had learnt since being at St. Swithin's that the best way to treat anything unusual was to ignore it, so I directed attention towards my new home.

The furniture in the sitting-room had an original touch which reflected the profession of the occupants. Like Axel Munthe's room in the Hôtel de l'Avenir, there were books everywhere. A row of them stood along the mantelpiece, from which the names of distin-

guished consultants could stare at the students in gold
lettering from red and black bindings, rebuking their
loose activities like a row of church elders. In the
window an uneven line of thick volumes ran along the
ledge like battlements. There were books on the floor,
dropped carelessly behind chairs or lost between pieces
of furniture and the wall. They were scattered over the
table like litter on a beach, mixed up with jam-pots,
pieces of bread, tobacco, newspapers, and beer bottles.
There was Price's famous *Medicine*, four inches thick,
with two thousand pages that told you about everything from measles to leprosy, from sore throat to heart
failure (it was also useful for propping open windows in
summer and supporting a reading lamp); there were
books on diabetes, appendicitis, bacteria, and bones;
books full of photographs of skin diseases, rashes, or
broken limbs; heavy dull books on pathology from
Scotland, with no more than a bare picture or two of a
growth or an ulcer to interrupt their closely-packed
print; books on obstetrics with line drawings of nonchalant babies being recovered from disquieting
predicaments; and scattered among them all like their
young were the thin little brown volumes of the
Students Aid series—an invaluable collection of
synopses that students fall back on, like compressed
emergency rations, when faced with imminent defeat
by the examiners. All this knowledge—all this
work, experience and advice from so many experts
—all the medical instruction in the world was
concentrated into a few square feet. It was ours for the
taking, if only we had ever sat down and started
reading.

A microscope stood in the corner, conveniently tilted
to take the eye, with an open wooden box of glass slides

beside it. The articulated bones of a hand lay on the table, mixed up with everything else. From the top of a cupboard in one corner a skull grinned down and provided a stand for a green hat with white cord round it that Benskin was sometimes moved to wear.

As well as this academic litter the room contained pieces of sports kit—rugger boots, woollen socks, a couple of cricket bats, and a dart-board on a splintered plywood backing. The occupants' leisure activities were also represented by a collection of signs, notices, and minor pieces of civic decoration that had from time to time been immorally carried off as trophies. It was a bad habit of St. Swithin's rugby team when playing away from home to pick up souvenirs of their visit before leaving, and in the course of seasons these had grown to a sizeable collection. There was a thirty-miles-limit sign in the corner and an orange beacon next to the skull on the cupboard. From a hook in the wall hung a policeman's helmet with the badge of the Cornwall Constabulary that had been carried off in a burst of vandalism at the end of a successful tour of the West Country. Below it a framed notice declared that the passing of betting slips was illegal, and on the opposite wall a board announcing the opening and closing times of the park. I discovered a little later that the bathroom door bore a metal notice saying 'Nurses Only,' and inside, at the appropriate place, was a small printed request not to use the adjacent apparatus while the train was standing at a station.

My inspection was interrupted by the reappearance of Vera. She was in her stockinged feet and wore only a skirt and a brassière which she was holding on with her hands.

'Richard, please do my bra up for me,' she asked. 'This damn fastener's gone wrong.'

She turned her slender shoulders.

'Thanks so much,' she said casually. She strolled back into her room and shut the door. I shrugged my shoulders and decided the only thing was to wait until the male members of the household arrived and guardedly discover Vera's precise function.

Vera, it turned out, was Archie's mistress. She was an Austrian girl, with an ensnaring personality and the ability to conduct herself towards her four sub-tenants with such graceful, impartial sisterliness that none of us would have thought of making advances towards her more than we could have contemplated committing incest. Besides, she did all the cooking and most of the little feminine odd jobs about the flat. This was appreciated as highly as her decorative qualities, for our own abilities in the kitchen did not go beyond baked beans and we were able to mend socks only by running a surgical purse-string suture round the hole and pulling it tight. Floor-scrubbing, fire-making, and the coarser domestic tasks were done by the men on a rough rota; but it was Vera who thought of buying a new shade for the lamp, ordering the coal, or telling one of us it was time to change his collar or have his hair cut.

Vera unfortunately had a bad habit of periodically upsetting the smooth running of the place by having sudden fierce quarrels with Archie which always ended by her packing up and leaving. Where she went to in these absences none of us knew. She had no relatives and no money, and Archie was so horrified at his own suspicion of how she maintained herself while she was away that he never dared to ask her outright. The flat

48

would become untidy and unscrubbed. The boiler would go out for lack of coal, and the five of us would nightly sit down to a progressively repellent supper of orange-coloured beans. In a week or so she would re-appear, as beautiful, as graceful, as sisterly as ever, throw herself into an orgy of reconciliation with Archie, and continue her household duties as if nothing had happened.

I floated contentedly into the drift of life in the flat. My companions treated the time-table of domestic life with contempt. They took meals when they were hungry, and if they felt like it sat up all night. Archie lived with Vera in a bed-sitting-room, and as they were an un-inhibited couple this afforded them sufficient privacy. His guests had the run of the rest of the place. We all shared the bathroom and, as we had to put shillings in the geyser, quite often the bath water as well. It was in connection with the bathroom that Vera became her most sisterly. She would walk in and start cleaning her teeth unruffled by a hairy male in the bath attempting to retain his modesty with the loofah. Although we were all far too gentlemanly knowingly to intrude while she was in the bath herself she was never worried by anyone bursting in. 'After all,' she would say flatteringly, 'you are all doctors.'

I felt I was living the true liberal life and developing my intellect, which were excuses for not settling down to the more concrete problems set by my text-books. The thought of the anatomy exam nevertheless hung over me uncomfortably, like the prospect of the eventual bill to a guest enjoying himself at a good hotel. One evening we discovered with a shock that the contest was only a month away, which gave Benskin and myself no alternative than cramming. We opened our text-books and drew a deep breath of knowledge, which we hoped we could hold until the examination was over. It was the worst time we could have chosen to start work. Mike Kelly had decided to learn the clarinet. Archie's landlord was trying to raise the rent, and Vera had disappeared again. On this occasion she never returned, and by the time the exam was held I was as miserable as her lover.

5

WHEN I heard I had passed the anatomy examination I felt like a man who had received an unexpected legacy. I had cut down my work preparing for the test by refusing to study at all topics that had been asked in the past few papers, in the belief that examiners, like lightning, never strike twice in the same place. I scraped into the pass list in company with Tony Benskin, John Bottle, Sprogget, Evans, and Harris. Grimsdyke also succeeded, and confessed himself amazed how near he must have come on previous occasions to the disaster of getting through.

I was elated: now I was released from the dull tyranny of the study of the dead in the dissecting room to the investigation of the dying in the hospital wards. I could start to perform like a real doctor; I could buy myself a stethoscope.

I strolled into a surgical instrument-maker's in Devonshire Street to select one, like a boy buying his first pipe. With the grave and critical air of a consultant cardiologist, I chose an impressive instrument with thick rubber tubes, a chest-piece as big as a jam-pot cover, and a few gadgets I could twiddle while delivering my professional opinions.

The choice was an important one, because in hospital

a stethoscope is as undisputable a sign of seniority as long trousers in a prep. school. It was not thought good taste to exhibit the instrument too blatantly, but a discreet length of tubing poking out of the coat, like a well-set pocket handkerchief, explained to your colleagues you had quitted the anatomy rooms for ever. With a bit of luck you might even be taken by the public for a real doctor. To the layman the stethoscope is the doctor's magic wand; if he sees a man with one round his neck he assumes he is a physician as readily as he takes a fellow in a clerical collar for a parson. These are a pair of conditioned reflexes that have from time to time been used for extracting small sums of money from well-meaning citizens by sufficiently respectable-looking confidence tricksters.

The next morning I walked proudly through the gates of St. Swithin's itself instead of going into the narrow door of the medical school. My first call was the student's lobby, to find which consultant I was appointed to.

Teaching of the clinical subjects—medicine, surgery, gynæcology, and midwifery—is carried on by a watered-down continuation of the old apprenticeship system. The year is divided into three-monthly terms, each of which the student spends attached to a different consultant. The doctor is the Chief, who usually takes on six or seven pupils known collectively as his firm, and dignified in the physician's wards with the title of medical clerks.

Each of the clerks is given four or five beds to look after. He is obliged to examine the patients admitted to them, write their notes, and scrape up an account of the case on the consultant's weekly list. Teaching is done at the bedside either by the Chief himself, his junior consultant, the registrar, or the houseman, and the students are expected to educate themselves in the intervals by nosing round the ward for instructive signs and symptoms and doing the unending medical odd jobs.

I began clinical work on a medical firm under the instruction of Dr. Malcolm Maxworth, M.D., F.R.C.P. Dr. Maxworth was one of the hospital's oldest physicians and had charge of male and female wards—Patience and Virtue. As he appeared only once a week the new students had to start by attending a small class given by the houseman on examination of the patient. We had at the time no more idea of the correct method for this than water-divining, and a Boy Scout with a first-aid certificate would have been more use in the wards than any of us.

The wards of St. Swithin's, which were contained in two large red-brick blocks, were dull, hostile galleries made up of a succession of irritating corners in which the nurses dusters flapped for ever in defiance. They were repeatedly being redecorated in an attempt to give them an air of modernity and cheerfulness, but the original design of the corridor-like rooms made fresh paint as ineffective as make-up on a crone. There was always a plan on foot to pull them down and rebuild, but the execution of this seemed to meet with baffling postponements. Meanwhile the staff took pride that they trod the same boards in the exercise of their art as their professional forebears, and the nurses spent a great deal of time they should have given to the patients sweeping the floors.

I walked across the court and up the dark stone stairs to Virtue ward. Tony Benskin, Grimsdyke, and Evans were already standing outside the heavy glass doors.

dangling their stethoscopes and trying not to appear a little in awe of their surroundings, like Oxford freshmen or new prisoners at Dartmoor. We greeted each other in low, church tones.

The houseman came jumping down the stairs three at a time. We stiffened ourselves, like sentries coming to attention. He shot straight past and through the ward door, without appearing to notice us. A moment later his head popped out again.

'Are you relatives waiting to see someone?' he asked. He caught sight of our proud stethoscopes. 'Oh, you're the new clerks, I suppose. Damn it! I'm far too busy to show you anything.'

He scratched his curly head. He was a pleasant-looking fellow, about three years older than ourselves.

'Look,' he went on cheerfully. 'Get a sheet of instructions from Sister Virtue and see how you get on examining a few patients. I've got a lumbar puncture and a couple of aspirations to do, but I'll give you a hand when I can.'

He disappeared again. The small glow of self-importance over our promotion was dimmed. Glancing nervously at one another we went through the doors into the ward.

The houseman had already disappeared behind some screens round a bed at the far end. One or two nurses were busy attending to the patients. The four of us stood by the door for ten minutes. No one took the slightest notice.

From a small door on one side of the ward the Sister appeared. She immediately bore down on our quartet.

'Get out!' she hissed savagely.

I had never seen a sister close to before. This unexpected proximity had the effect of being in a rowing-boat under the bows of the *Queen Mary*.

Sister Virtue was a fine body of a woman. She was about six feet tall, her figure was as burly as a policeman's, and she advanced on her adversaries with two belligerent breasts. Even her broad bottom as she passed looked as formidable as the stern of a battleship. Her dress was speckless blue and her apron as crisp as a piece of paper. She had a face like the side of a quarry and wore a fine grey moustache.

My immediate impulse was to turn and run screaming down the stairs. Indeed, all of us jumped back anxiously, as if afraid she might bite. But we stood our ground.

'We're the new clerks,' I mumbled in a dry voice.

She looked at us as if we were four unpleasant objects some patient had just brought up.

'I won't have any nonsense here,' she said abruptly. 'None at all.'

We nodded our heads briskly, indicating that nonsense of any sort was not contemplated.

'You're not to come in the ward after twelve o'clock, in the afternoons, or after six in the evening. Understand?'

Her eyes cauterized each of us in turn.

'And you're not to interfere with the nurses.'

Grimsdyke raised an eyebrow.

'Don't be cheeky!' she snapped.

She turned quickly to her desk and came back with some foolscap sheets of typewritten notes.

'Take these,' she commanded.

We selected a sheet each. They were headed 'Instructions on Case-Taking for Students.'

'You may look at patients number five, eight, twelve,

and twenty,' Sister Virtue went on sternly. 'You will replace the bedclothes neatly. You will always ask the staff nurse for a chaperon before examining any female patient below the head and neck. Kindly remember that I do not like students in my ward at all, but we are forced to put up with you.'

Her welcome finished, she spun round and sailed off to give a probationer hell for not dusting the window-ledges the correct way.

We silently crept through the doors and leant against the wall of the corridor outside to read the instruction papers. Grimsdyke was the only one to speak.

'I wonder if she goes to lunch on a broomstick?' he said.

I turned my thoughts to the typewritten paper. 'A careful history must be taken before the patient is examined,' I read. There followed a list of things to ask. It started off easily enough—'Name. Address. Age. Marital state. Occupation. For how long? Does he like it?' It continued with a detailed interrogation on the efficiency with which the patient performed every noticeable physiological function from coughing to coitus.

I turned the page over. The other side was headed 'Examination.' I read half-way down, but I was burning to try my luck on a real patient. I stuffed the paper in my pocket, like a child tossing aside the instructions for working a new complicated toy. I carefully put my nose inside the door and was relieved to find Sister had returned to her lair. I thought she was probably digesting someone.

Timidly I walked down the rows of beds to patient number twelve.

'Look where you're going!' a female voice said angrily in my ear.

I spun round. Behind me was a cross-looking nurse. She was young and not bad-looking, and she wore the bows and blue belt of a qualified staff-nurse.

'Can't you see that floor has just been polished?' she demanded.

'I'm sorry,' I mumbled. She tossed her head and stalked off with a swish of starched apron.

Number twelve was a stout young blonde browning at the roots—a frequent condition in female wards. She was sitting up in bed in a green woollen jacket reading a book by Peter Cheyney.

'Good morning,' I said humbly, expecting she as well would attack me.

She immediately slipped a piece of paper in her book, set it down on her bedside locker, threw off her bed-jacket, and dropped the top of her nightdress off her shoulders to reveal a large and not unpleasant bosom. Then she smiled.

'Good morning,' she said. She was obviously used to the routine.

I felt a little at a loss. I had never been in such circumstances before, anywhere.

'Er—do you mind if I examine you?' I asked diffidently.

'Go ahead,' she said invitingly, giving me a bigger smile.

'Thanks awfully.'

The experience was so unusual I couldn't think of anything to say. I groped for remembrance of the instructions, but the sheets in my mind's eye were as blank as the patient's counterpane. I felt like an after-dinner speaker who had risen to his feet and found he'd forgotten his notes. Then an idea rescued me unexpectedly—I would take her pulse. Seizing one wrist, I felt for the throbbing radial artery while I gazed with unseeing concentration at the face of my wrist-watch. I felt I had held her arm for five minutes or more, wondering what to do next. And all the time her gently heaving breasts kept tugging at my eyes. They fascinated me, not with any sexual appeal but alarmingly, as if they were a couple of dangerous snakes. I noticed they had fine drops of sweat on them near the nipples.

A thought exploded in my mind.

'I must fetch a nurse!' I exclaimed. I dropped her wrist as if she had smallpox. 'A chaperone, you know.'

She giggled.

'Oh, go on with you!' she said playfully.

I backed away quickly. A nurse undecorated with belts or bows was dusting a locker on the other side of the ward. She looked hearteningly junior.

'I wonder if you would kindly chaperone me with a patient for a few minutes?' I asked urgently.

'No!' she said. She paused in her dusting to glance at me. I must have looked so miserable a little pity glowed in her heart. 'Ask the junior probationer,' she suggested brusquely. 'It's her job. She's in the sluice-room cleaning the bedpans.'

I thanked her humbly and went to look for my helpmeet. She was a worried-looking girl of about eighteen who was busy polishing a pile of metal bedpans as if they were the family silver.

'Will you please be my chaperone?' I asked meekly.

She pushed a lock of straw-coloured hair out of her eyes wearily.

'I suppose so,' she said. 'If I have to.'

We went back into the ward together and gathered

some screens round the stout blonde's bed. The probationer stood opposite me with a look of contempt on her face for my inexpert manipulations while I examined the blonde's tongue, her eyes, and her teeth. I stuck my stethoscope warily here and there on her chest, though the noises were as uninformative to my ears as the sound of sea on a distant shore.

Taking the earpieces out I said 'Good!' as if I had completed my diagnosis.

'Aren't you going to examine my tummy?' asked the blonde with disappointment. 'All the doctors examine my tummy. It's my tummy what's wrong.'

'To-morrow,' I said firmly. 'I have to go and operate.'

How could I tell her in front of the nurse I had not yet learned as far as the tummy?

*　　*　　*　　*　　*

Inspection, palpation, percussion, auscultation—the unalterable, ever-applicable tetrad. They were drummed into us like drill to recruits. Whatever part of the patient you examine, whatever disease you suspect, the four motions must be gone through in that order. You look first, then feel; when you have felt, you may tap, but not before; and last of all comes the stethoscope.

I began to learn how to look at a patient so that even the fingernails might shine with a dozen diagnoses. They taught us to feel lumps, livers, and spleens; how to percuss correctly and to understand the evasive murmurs transmitted through a stethoscope. Diagnosis is simple observation and applied logic—detection, in fact. A matter of searching for clues, igniting a suspicion and knowing where to look for proof. Conan Doyle

59

modelled Sherlock Holmes on a physician, and the reverse holds perfectly well.

Dr. Maxworth took his firm round the ward every Wednesday morning. He was a thin, desiccated little man who had never been known to appear in public dressed in anything but black coat and striped trousers. He was not really interested in students at all. For most of the round he forgot we were crowding in his footsteps, and would suddenly recall our presence by throwing a few half-audible scraps of instruction over his shoulder. He was a specialist in neurology, the diseases of the nervous system. This is the purest and most academic branch of medicine and requires for its practice a mind capable of playing three games of chess simultaneously while filling in a couple of stiff crossword puzzles between the moves. As almost all the nervous diseases we saw in the ward appeared to be fatal, it seemed to me a pretty barren speciality. But Maxworth drew exquisite pleasure from it. He was not primarily concerned with treating his patients and making them better, but if he scored a diagnosis before the proof of the post-mortem he was delighted. He was, his houseman said, a fairly typical physician.

I began to see how the ward was managed by Sister, whom I avoided like a pile of radium. Every bodily occurrence that could be measured—the pulse, the amount of urine, the quantity of vomit, the number of baths—was carefully entered against the patient's name in the treatment book, which reduced the twenty or so humans in the ward to a daily row of figures in her aggressive handwriting.

There were two functions of the physiology which Sister thought proceeded wholly in her interest. One was temperature. The temperature charts shone neatly from the foot of the beds, and each showed a precise horizontal zigzag of different amplitude. Sister wrote the dots and dashes on them herself every morning and evening. The temperatures were taken by the junior nurses, who used four or five thermometers. In spite of inaccuracies due to a different instrument being used daily on each patient and the varying impatience of the nurse to whip the glass spicule away, the figures were looked upon as indispensable. Any errors occurring through mercurial or human failings were not of great importance, however, because Sister always substituted figures of her own if the ones returned by the patient did not fit with her notion of what the temperature in the case ought to be.

The other particular concern of the Sister was the patient's bowels. A nurse was sent round the ward every evening with a special book to ask how many times each inmate had performed during the past twenty-four hours. 'How many for the book?' she would enquire with charming coyness. The patients caught the spirit of the thing, and those returning fair scores to the nurse did so with a proud ring in their voices but anyone making a duck confessed with shame and cowered under the bedclothes.

The number of occasions was written in a separate square at the foot of the temperature chart. A nought was regarded by Sister as unpleasant, and more than two blank days she took as a personal insult. Treatment was simple. One nought was allowed to pass without punishment, but two automatically meant cascara, three castor oil, and four the supreme penalty of an enema.

We rapidly became accustomed to our position of inferiority to everyone on the ward staff. Like all apprentices, the students were used as cheap labour by their superiors. We did all the medical chores—urine-testing, gruel meals in patients with duodenal ulcers, blood samples, and a few simple investigations. For the first few weeks everything seemed easy. It was only at the end of the three-month appointment that there crept up on me an uneasy certainty that I did not yet even know enough to realize how ignorant I was.

6

THE impact of surgery on the student is likely to be more dramatic than the first gentle touch of medicine. Although surgeons have now abandoned such playful habits as hurling a freshly amputated leg at a newcomer in the theatre, the warm, humid atmosphere, the sight of blood spilt with apparent carelessness, and the first view of human intestines laid out like a string of new sausages sometimes induces in a student a fit of the vapours—a misfortune which draws from his unaffected companions the meagre sympathy afforded a seasick midshipman.

Nevertheless, I started the surgical course with a feeling of superiority over my predecessors of ten or fifteen years ago. As I went to the pictures fairly regularly I was already as familiar with the inside of an operating theatre as with my father's consulting room. From a seat in the local cinema not only myself but most other people in the country had achieved a thorough and painless knowledge of what went on behind the doors marked 'Sterile.' I was ready for it all: the crisp white gowns; the cool, unhurried efficiency; the tense concentrated silence broken only by the click of instruments, a curt word of command from the surgeon, or a snapped-out demand for a fresh ligature by the theatre sister. I prepared myself to face the

solemnity of an operation, with the attention of everyone in the room focused on the unconscious patient
like the strong beam of the operating spotlight.

I was attached to Sir Lancelot Spratt for my surgical
teaching. My official title was Sir Lancelot's dresser,
which meant not that I had to help him into his white
operating trousers in the surgeons' changing-room, but
that I was supposed to be responsible for the daily
dressings of three or four patients in the ward. The
name had a pleasing dignity about it and suggested the
student really did something useful in the hospital
instead, as it was always impressed on him by the
nurses and houseman, of getting in everyone's way like
a playful kitten.

The appointment of Sir Lancelot's firm was something of an honour, as he was the Senior Surgeon of the
hospital and one of its best-known figures. He was a tall,
bony, red-faced man with a bald head round which a
ring of white fluffy hair hung like clouds at a mountain
top. He was always perfectly shaved and manicured and
wore suits cut with considerably more skill than many
of his own incisions. He was on the point of retiring
from the surgical battlefield on which he had won and
lost (with equal profit) so many spectacular actions,
and he was always referred to by his colleagues in after-
dinner speeches and the like as 'a surgeon of the grand
old school.' In private they gave him the less charming
but equivalent epithet of 'that bloody old butcher.' His
students were fortunate in witnessing operations in his
theatre of an extent and originality never seen else-
where. Nothing was too big for him to cut out, and no
viscus, once he had formed an impression it was
exercising some indefinite malign influence on the
patient, would remain for longer than a week *in situ*.

Sir Lancelot represented a generation of colourful, energetic surgeons that, like fulminating cases of scarlet fever, are rarely seen in hospital wards to-day. He inherited the professional aggression of Liston, Paget, Percival Pott, and Moynihan, for he was trained in the days when the surgeon's slickness was the only hope of the patient's recovery, the days before complicated anæsthetics, penicillin, blood-transfusion, and the other paraphernalia of modern surgery had watered down the operator's skill and threatened to submerge him completely.

Sir Lancelot had made a fortune, chiefly from the distressing complaints of old gentlemen, and was charging two hundred guineas for an appendicectomy while Aneurin Bevan was still thumping a local tub in Ebbw Vale. His real success started in the 'twenties, when he earned his knighthood by performing a small but essential operation on a cabinet minister that allowed him to take his seat in the House with greater ease. The minister was delighted, and recommended him in every drawing-room of importance in London. Just at that time Sir Lancelot got it into his head that rheumatism could be cured by the removal from the body of all organs not strictly necessary for the continuance of life. As most people over the age of fifty have rheumatism and it is impossible to make it much better or much worse with any form of treatment his practice increased tenfold overnight.

The rheumatism rage lasted long enough for him to buy a house in Harley Street, a country home on the Thames, a cottage in Sussex, a small sailing yacht, and a new Rolls, in which he was still wafted round between the four of them and the hospital. By then he was ready to operate on anything—he was, he told his dressers with pride, one of the last of the general surgeons. He claimed to be capable of removing a stomach or a pair of tonsils with equal success, or to be able to cut off a leg or a lung.

Every Tuesday and Thursday afternoon he operated in his own theatre on the top floor. The list for the session was pinned up outside like a music-hall bill— the best cases were always at the top for Sir Lancelot to operate on himself, and the programme degenerated into a string of such minor surgical chores as the repair of hernias and the removal of varicose veins, to be done by his assistants when he had gone off to his club for a glass of sherry before dinner.

On the first Tuesday after my appointment to the firm I walked up the stairs to the theatre—students were not allowed to use the hospital lift—and went into the dressers' changing-room. A row of jackets and ties hung under a notice in letters three inches high: DO NOT LEAVE ANYTHING IN YOUR POCKETS. Everyone entering the theatre had to wear sterile clothing, which was packed away in three metal bins opened by foot pedals. Using a pair of long sterile forceps I took an oblong cap from one, a mask from another, and a rolled white gown from the third. Unfortunately there was no indication of the size of these coverings, and the gown fell round my feet like a bridal dress while the cap perched on my head like a cherry on a dish of ice-cream. I pushed open the theatre door and stepped inside reverently, like a tourist entering a cathedral. Standing by the door, my hands clasped tightly behind me, all I wanted was completely to escape notice. I felt that even my breathing, which sounded in my ears like the bellows of a church organ, would disturb the sterile, noiseless efficiency of the place. I was also a little uncertain of my reactions to cut flesh and wanted to keep as far away from the scene of activity as possible.

'You, boy!'

Sir Lancelot's head popped above the caps of his attendants. All I could see of him was a single brown, bushy strip that separated the top of his mask and the edge of his cap, through which there glared two un-friendly eyes like a hungry tiger inspecting a native through the undergrowth.

'Come over here,' he shouted. 'How often have I got to tell you young fellers you can't learn surgery from the door-post?'

The operating table was in the centre of the bare, tiled room, directly under the wide lamp that hung like a huge inverted saucer from the ceiling. It was com-pletely invisible, as about twenty figures in white gowns were packed round it like tube passengers in the rush-hour. These were mostly students. The operating team was made up of Sir Lancelot himself, who was a head higher than anyone else in the room; his theatre Sister, masked and with all her hair carefully tucked into a sterile white turban, standing on a little platform beside him; his senior houseman, Mr. Stubbins, and his registrar, Mr. Crate, assisting him from the opposite side; and his anæsthetist, sitting on a small metal piano stool beside a chromium-plated barrow of apparatus at the head of the table, reading the *Daily Telegraph*. On the outskirts of this scrum two nurses in sterile clothes dashed round anxiously, dishing out hot sterilized instruments from small metal bowls like waiters serving spaghetti. A theatre porter, also gowned and masked, leant reflectively on a sort of towel rail used for counting the swabs, and another strode in with a fresh cylinder of oxygen on his shoulder. The only indication that there was a patient present at all was a pair of feet in thick, coarse-knitted bed-socks that stuck pathetically from one end of the audience.

As soon as Sir Lancelot spoke, the group round the table opened as if he were Aladdin at the mouth of his cave. I walked unhappily into the centre. My companions closed tightly behind me, and I found myself wedged against the table opposite Sir Lancelot with a man who played in the second row of the hospital forwards immediately behind me. Escape was therefore out of the question, on physical as well as moral grounds.

The operation was on the point of starting. The patient was still invisible, as the body was covered with sterile towels except for a clean-shaved strip of lower abdomen on the right-hand side of which the operating light was focused diagnostically. I couldn't even see if it was a young man or a woman.

Having forced me into a ringside seat, Sir Lancelot then appeared to dismiss me from his mind. He paused to adjust the cuff of the rubber glove that stretched over his bony hand. Stubbins and Crate were waiting with gauze dabs, and the theatre sister was threading needles with catgut as unconcernedly as if she was going to darn her stockings.

'Stubbins,' said Sir Lancelot chattily, making a three-inch incision over the appendix, 'remind me to look into Fortnum's on my way home, there's a good lad. My missus'll give me hell if I forget her dried ginger again. I suppose it was all right for me to start?' he asked the anæsthetist.

The *Daily Telegraph* rustled slightly in assent.

I was surprised. Dried ginger in an operating theatre?

Shopping lists disturbing the sanctity of surgery? And the *Daily Telegraph*?

'I've got a damn funny story to tell you lads,' went on Sir Lancelot affably, deepening his incision. 'Make you all laugh. Happened to me last week. An old lady turned up in my rooms in Harley Street . . . Sister!' he exclaimed in a tone of sudden annoyance, 'do you expect me to operate with a jam-spreader? This knife's a disgrace.'

He threw it on the floor. Without looking at him she handed him another.

'That's better,' Sir Lancelot growled. Then, in his previous tone, as though he were two people making conversation, he went on: 'Where was I? Oh yes, the old lady. Well, she said she'd come to see me on the advice of Lord—Lord Someoneorother, I can't remember these damn titles—whom I'd operated on last year. She said she was convinced she'd got gallstones.

'Now look here, Stubbins, can't you and Crate keep out of each other's way? Your job is to use that gauze swab sensibly, not wave it around like a Salvation Army banner. How the devil do you think I can operate properly if everything's wallowing in blood? Why am I always cursed with assistants who have a couple of left hands? And I want a clip, Sister. Hurry up, woman, I can't wait all night!'

Sir Lancelot had cut through the abdominal wall while he was talking, like a child impatient to see inside a Christmas parcel.

'Well,' he went on, all affability again, seemingly conducting the operation with the concentration of a gossipy woman knitting a pair of socks, 'I said to this old lady, "Gallstones, eh? Now, my dear, what makes you think you've got gallstones?" And I've never seen anyone look so embarrassed in my life!'

He returned to the operation.

'What's this structure, gentlemen?'

A reply came from under a student's mask on the edge of the crowd.

'Quite correct, whoever you are,' said Sir Lancelot, but without any congratulation in his voice. 'Glad to see you fellers remember a little fundamental anatomy from your two years in the rooms . . . so I wondered what was up. After all, patients don't get embarrassed over gallstones. It's only piles and things like that, and even then it's never the old ladies who are coy but the tough young men. Remember that bit of advice, gentlemen. . . . Come on, Stubbins, wake up! You're as useless as an udder on a bull.'

He produced the appendix from the wound like a bird pulling a worm from the ground, and laid it and the attached intestine on a little square of gauze.

'Then the old lady said to me, "As a matter of fact, Sir Lancelot, I've been passing them all month. . . ." Don't lean on the patient, Stubbins! If I'm not tired you shouldn't be, and I can give you forty or fifty years, my lad.

'So now we come to the interesting part of the story. She showed me a little box, like those things you send out pieces of wedding cake in. . . . Sister! What in the name of God are you threading your needles with? This isn't catgut, it's rope. What's that, woman?' He leant the red ear that stuck out below his cap towards her. 'Speak up, don't mutter to yourself. I'm not being rude, damn you! I'm never rude in the theatre. All right, tell your Matron, but give us a decent ligature. That's more like it. Swab, man, swab. Stubbins, did I ever tell you about the Matron when she was a junior theatre nurse? She had a terrible crush on a fellow house-surgeon of mine—chap called Bungo Ross, used to drink like a fish and a devil for the women. Became a respected G.P. in Bognor or somewhere. Died last year. I wrote a damn good obituary for him in the *British Medical Journal*. I'm tying off the appendicular artery, gentlemen. See? What's that, Stubbins? Oh, the old lady. Cherry stones.'

He tossed the appendix into a small enamel bowl held for him by Stubbins.

'Looks a bit blue this end, George,' he said in the direction of the anæthetist. 'All right, I suppose?' The anæsthetist was at the time in the corner of the theatre talking earnestly to one of the nurses who had been serving out the instruments. Theatre kit is unfair to nurses; it makes them look like white bundles. But one could tell from the rough shape of this one, from the little black-stockinged ankles below her gown and the two wide eyes above her mask, that the parcel would be worth the unwrapping. The anæsthetist jumped back to his trolley and began to twiddle the knobs on it. Sister, who was already in a wild temper, injected the nurse with a glance like a syringeful of strychnine.

'Forceps, Sister!' bellowed Sir Lancelot. She handed him a pair which he looked at closely, snapping them together in front of his mask. For some reason they displeased him, so he threw them over the heads of the crowd at the opposite wall. This caused no surprise to anyone, and seemed to be one of his usual habits. She calmly handed him another pair.

'Swabs correct, Sister, before I close? Good. Terribly important that, gentlemen. Once you've left a swab inside a patient you're finished for life. Courts, damages, newspapers, and all that sort of thing. It's the only disaster in surgery the blasted public thinks it knows anything about. Cut their throats when they're under the anæsthetic, yes, but leave anything inside and you're in the *News of the World* in no time. Shove in the skin stitches, Stubbins. What's the next case? Tea? Excellent. Operating always makes me thirsty.'

7

DURING the following three months I learnt a
little about surgery and a lot about surgeons.
I learnt more than I wanted about Sir Lancelot.
In the theatre he was God. Everything in the routine
for operating sessions was arranged to suit his con-
venience. A white linen suit, freshly starched, was
carefully warmed by the junior nurse before being
laid out in his changing-room in the morning. A
Thermos pitcher of iced water labelled 'Sir Lancelot
Spratt ONLY' was set on a silver tray nearby. He had
his own masks, his own scrubbing brush, and his own
soap. When he crossed the theatre floor from the scrub-
up basins to the table the onlookers scattered before
him like unarmed infantry in front of a tank. If anyone
got in his way he simply kicked them out of it. He rarely
asked for an instrument but expected the Sister to guess
which one to place in his waiting hand. If she made a
mistake, he calmly dropped the wrong instrument on
to the floor. Should she do no better at her second
attempt he repeated his little trick. Once he silently
reduced a whole trayful of instruments to an unsterile
heap at his feet, and the Sister had hysterics.

Sir Lancelot had a personality like an avalanche and
a downright bedside manner that suited equally well a
duchess's bedroom or the hospital out-patient depart-

ment. He radiated confidence like a lighthouse through a storm. His suggestions on the removal of his patients' organs never met with their objection. The more he did to them, the greater the complications that resulted from his interference, the larger the number of supplementary operations he had to perform to retrieve his errors, the more they thanked him: there was never one but died grateful.

His teaching in the ward, like his surgery in the theatre, was full-blooded. He had a long string of aphorisms and surgical anecdotes, none of which was original or strictly accurate, but they stuck in the minds of his students long after the watery lectures of his colleagues had evaporated.

His round was held every Tuesday morning at ten o'clock, and had the same effect on the ward as an admiral's inspection of a small warship.

The preparations for his visit began about five in the morning. The night nurses started the long business of sprucing up the ward to its best pitch of speckless sterility; and when Sister and her day staff arrived at seven the energy given to preparing the long room so that nothing in the slightest way offensive should fall on the great man's eye was increased tenfold. Every article in it was scrubbed and polished thoroughly—the floor, the medicine cupboards, the windows, the instruments, the patients' faces. The bedside lockers, which usually carried a friendly jumble of newspapers, soap, jam, football coupons, and barley-water, were stripped clean and their contents buried out of sight. Even the flowers looked sterile.

The tension and activity in the ward rose together, like the temperature and pulse in a fever. At nine the senior house-surgeon, in a fresh white jacket, looked in for a worried, whispered conversation with Sister to be certain everything commanded on the Chief's last visit had been done. He didn't glance at the patients. That morning they were part of the ward furniture, or at most instruments by which the medical staff could demonstrate their abilities to Sir Lancelot.

There was one point, however, on which the patients could not be argued away from their humanity. At nine-fifteen bedpans were issued all round. The acquisition of one of these at such an hour (seven and five were the official times for their use) was usually a business comparable with catching the eye of a waiter in a busy restaurant. At nine-fifteen on Tuesdays, however, they were forced upon the patients. The nurses tripped briskly out of the sluice-room, each carrying a couple under a cloth. This was because Sister thought a request for one of these articles while Sir Lancelot was in the ward unreasonable to the highest degree—indeed, almost indecent.

The bedpans were whipped away a quarter of an hour before the Chief was due. There followed an energetic final ten minutes occupied by a process known as 'tidying' the patients. They could obviously not be allowed to disturb the general symmetry of the scene by lolling about in bed anyhow, like a squad of soldiers falling in with their hands in their pockets. They had to be fitted in to the ward neatly and unobtrusively. The technique was simple. A pair of nurses descended on the patient. First he was shot into the sitting position, and retained there by one nurse while the other smoothed and squared up his pillows (the open ends of the pillow-cases always to face away from the door). He was then dropped gently on his back, so as not to ruffle the smooth surface unnecessarily with his head. The bedclothes were seized at the top by the two young women and pulled taut between them like a tug-of-war; they next applied the tension upwards from the patient's feet, which brought the top edge of the bedclothes level with the patient's nostrils. In one quick motion, without releasing the tension to which the blankets were submitted, they tucked them in firmly all round. This made it impossible for the occupant of the bed to perform any muscular movement whatever, except very shallow breathing.

The ward by ten was silent, orderly, and odourless. Sister and the nurses had changed into fresh white aprons and each of them felt like Moses immediately on his arrival at the top of the mountain. Meanwhile, another focus of consternation had formed not far away.

It was the tradition of St. Swithin's that the Chief should be greeted in the courtyard and lead his firm to the ward. Surgeons were met in front of the statue of Sir Benjamin Bone and physicians before that of Lord Larrymore. This form of reception resulted in everyone becoming cold in winter, hot in summer, and wet all the year round, and as it had apparently been going on for three or four hundred years this seemed an excellent reason for refusing to alter it.

We gathered for our first ward-round under the cold eye of Sir Benjamin. The differences that divided the firm, which were emphasised on Tuesday mornings, had already become obvious. The students stood in a little subdued group behind the statue. We wore our suits, with stethoscopes coiling out of our pockets and foolscap notebooks under our arms. We chatted quietly between ourselves, but would not have contemplated exchanging words with the two house-surgeons, who stood apart murmuring to each other with expressions of intense seriousness on their faces.

The third section of the party consisted only of Crate, the registrar. He was allowed to wear a long white coat like the Chief, but as he had no companion to talk to and was unable to converse with his housemen or students at such a solemn moment he had to content himself with looking at the sky in a reflective and earnest way, as if he were turning over in his mind the niceties of surgery or trying to forecast the weather.

At ten the Rolls drew into the courtyard and stopped opposite our group. Crate opened the door and wished Sir Lancelot good morning. The car was driven to its parking-place by the chauffeur and the Chief disappeared with his registrar towards the staff common room to leave his hat and put on his white coat. When they reappeared the rest of the party followed them to the wards.

Once Sir Lancelot burst through the ward door more people arranged themselves in his wake. Indeed, it was impossible for a man of his importance to walk about St. Swithin's at all without a procession immediately forming up behind him.

First, of course, was Sir Lancelot, the therapeutic thunderbolt. A pace behind came the registrar, and behind him the two house-surgeons, the senior one leading. After the two housemen was Sister, her long cap trailing behind her like a wind-stocking on an aerodrome. She was followed by her senior staff nurse, who carried a trayful of highly-polished instruments with which the patients could be tapped, scratched, and tickled in the aid of making a diagnosis. Sir Lancelot never used any of them and probably did not know how to, but they were produced every Tuesday

77

nevertheless, like a ceremonial mace. Behind the staff nurse was a junior nurse bearing a thick board covered with a pad of paper, to which a pencil was attached with a piece of string. The board was marked sternly 'SIR LANCELOT SPRATT'S DRAWING PAPER.' On this he would sometimes sketch points of anatomy—not often, about once every six months, but the board had to be flashed to his hand if he asked for it. In the rear of the junior nurse, in the winter months a probationer carried a hot-water bottle in a small red blanket for Sir Lancelot to warm his hands before applying them to exposed flesh.

At the end of the party, behind even the hot-water bottle, were the students: an un-uniformed, disorderly bunch of stragglers.

The Chief spent two hours examining the candidates for the afternoon's operating list, with whom he illustrated to us the principles of surgery. Sometimes he passed all morning on one case, if the patient contained a lump of sufficient interest to him; on other Tuesdays he would whip round the whole ward, diagnosing like a machine-gun. Sitting was forbidden, and towards lunchtime the students shifted heavily from one foot to the other. Sir Lancelot thought any young man incapable of standing on his own feet for a couple of hours as another disagreeable product of modern life, like socialism.

On our first ward round we were pushed easily into place by the precision with which the rest of the troupe fell in. Sir Lancelot strode across the ward, drew up sharply, and looked over the patients in the two rows of beds, sniffing the air like a dog picking up a scent. He thundered over to the bedside of a small, nervous man in the corner. The firm immediately rearranged itself, like a smart platoon at drill. The Chief towered on the right of the patient's head; Sister stood opposite, her nurses squeezed behind her; the students surrounded the foot and sides of the bed like a screen; and the registrar and housemen stood beyond them, at a distance indicating that they were no longer in need of any instruction in surgery.

Sir Lancelot pulled back the bedclothes like a conjurer revealing a successful trick.

'You just lie still, old fellow,' he boomed cheerfully at the patient. 'Don't you take any notice of what I'm going to say to these young doctors. You won't understand a word of what we're talking about, anyway. Take his pyjamas off, Sister. Now you, my boy,' he continued, gripping me tightly by the arm as I was nearest, 'take a look at that abdomen.'

I stretched out a hand to feel the patient gingerly in the region of the umbilicus. I noticed his skin was covered with goose-pimples and twitched here and there nervously.

'Take your dirty little hand away!' said Sir Lancelot savagely, flicking it off the surface of the abdomen like a fly. He paused solemnly, and continued in a heavy tone, wagging his finger: 'The first rule of surgery, gentlemen—eyes first and most, hands next and least, tongue not at all. Look first and don't chatter. An excellent rule for you to remember all your lives. Now look, boy, look.'

I gazed at the abdomen for a whole minute but it appeared no different from any that might be seen on Brighton beach. When I thought I had inspected it long enough to satisfy the Chief, who rose uncomfortably above me, I diffidently stretched out my arm and prodded about with my finger in search of a lump.

'*Doucemong, doucemong,*' Sir Lancelot began again. 'Gently, boy—you're not making bread. Remember'—his finger came up again warningly—'a successful surgeon must have the eye of a hawk, the heart of a lion, and the hand of a lady.'

'And the commercial morals of a Levantine usurer,' murmured Grimsdyke under his breath.

With a glow of relief, I finally discovered the lump. It was about the size of an orange and tucked under the edge of the ribs. We lined up and felt it one after the other, while Sir Lancelot looked on closely and corrected anyone going about it the wrong way. Then he pulled a red grease-pencil from the top pocket of his coat and handed it to me.

'Where are we going to make the incision?' he asked. By now the patient was forgotten; it was the lump we were after. Sir Lancelot had an upsetting habit of treating the owners of lumps as if they were already rendered unconscious by the anæsthetic.

I drew a modest line over the lesion.

'Keyhole surgery!' said Sir Lancelot with contempt. 'Damnable! Give me the pencil!' He snatched it away. 'This, gentlemen, will be our incision.'

He drew a broad, decisive, red sweep from the patient's ribs to below his umbilicus.

'We will open the patient like *that*. Then we can have a good look inside. It's no good rummaging round an abdomen if you can't get your hand in comfortably. What do we do then? Right—take a better look at the lump we've been feeling. Do you think it's going to be easy to remove?' he asked me, gripping my arm again.

'No, sir.'

'Correct—it's going to be most difficult. And dangerous. There are at least a dozen ways in which we can make a slight error—even though we are experienced surgeons—and kill the patient like that!' He snapped his fingers frighteningly.

'Now!' He tapped the abdomen with his pencil as if knocking for admission. 'When we have cut through the skin what is the next structure we shall meet? Come on, you fellers. You've done your anatomy more recently than I have . . . what's that? Yes, subcutaneous fat. Then, gentlemen, we first encounter the surgeon's worst enemy.' He glared at us all in turn. 'What?' he demanded in general. There was no reply. 'Blood!' he thundered.

At that point the patient restored his personality to the notice of his doctors by vomiting.

*　　*　　*　　*　　*

Surgery was Sir Lancelot's life and St. Swithin's was his home. He had given more of his time for nothing to the hospital than he ever used to make his fortune. He was president or vice-president of almost every students' club and supported the rugby team from the touchline in winter with the same roar he used on ignorant dressers in the theatre. During the war he slept every night at the hospital in the bombing, and operated on casualties in an improvised theatre in the basement as long as they came in. A team of students lived in as well and he used to play cards with them or share a pint of beer, actions which at first caused as much dismay as if he had arrived to operate in his underpants. One night St. Swithin's was hit while he was operating. The theatre rocked, the lights went out, and part of the ceiling fell in. But Sir Lancelot simply swore and went on—bombs to him were just another irritation in surgery, like fumbling assistants and blunt knives, and he treated them all the same way.

The only time Sir Lancelot became at all subdued was when he talked of his retirement. It hung over him all the time I was on his firm. The prospect of losing his two days a week at St. Swithin's depressed him, though he was cheered by remembering that the hospital would immediately acknowledge him as an emeritus consultant and perhaps call him in for cases of supreme difficulty. His connection with St. Swithin's would therefore not be completely broken; he could go on meeting the students at their clubs, and as for surgery he could continue that in private.

One day, shortly after I left his firm, he disappeared. He said good-bye to no one. He left his work to his assistant and wrote a note to the Chairman of the Governors simply stating he would not be in again. The hospital radiologist explained it later with an X-ray film. Sir Lancelot had a cancer in his stomach and had gone off to his cottage in Sussex to die. He refused to have an operation.

8

THE Nurses' Home at St. Swithin's was known, with a fair degree of accuracy, as the Virgins' Retreat. Virginity and nursing certainly seem to go together, and the Matron of St. Swithin's put her Ursulian duties first. Her regulations for the nurses' conduct suggested she was convinced they went through their waking and sleeping life at the hospital in unremitting danger of rape. It is true that a student or two occasionally entertained sinful thoughts towards one of her charges; like any other bunch of young men they were romantic souls, and the fact that young ladies took off their clothes for them in the wards did not deter them from trying for the same result in their lodgings. But, taking the nurses as a whole, their Matron's book of rules was nothing more than a blatant piece of flattery.

Intercourse between the nurses and students had to be but social to attract the Matron's displeasure. If a nurse was seen talking to a student in the hospital, apart from a brief necessary exchange of medical matters in the ward, she was dismissed unquestioned. For her to meet a student in her off-duty time—to go to the pictures or a concert, for instance—was automatically reckoned, if discovered, as the equivalent of a week-end in Brighton. And if a nurse was found in the students'

quarters or a man of any sort discovered in the Nurses'
Home it was an event apparently unmeasurable in
terms of human horror.

In order to reduce the possibility of these alarming
situations overtaking the nurse the opportunities she
could present for them were heavily reduced. All first-
year nurses had to be in by ten every night. The senior
girls were allowed out once a week until eleven, and
staff nurses were permitted in comparison a life of
uninhibited lechery by being able to claim two weekly
passes until twelve.

Nurses, when in the hospital, were authoritatively
stripped of their sexual characteristics as far as was
possible without operative interference. Make-up of any
sort was looked upon by the ward sisters as the preroga-
tive of women of the streets, and hair was supposed to
be tightly tucked inside a starched uniform cap
designed to be worn just over the eyebrows. The nurse's
figure was de-contoured beneath uniform made out of
a material similar to sailcloth, and the skirt was raised
only far enough from the floor to let the poor girl walk
without breaking her neck.

These regulations were naturally broken, as efficiently
and as subtly as the lock on a medieval chastity belt.
There were plenty of quiet corners about the hospital
where a date could be arranged between student and
nurse, and the couple had the whole of London to meet
in. A thin, skilful brush with a lipstick could bring even
from Sister Virtue nothing worse than suspicion and
powder was almost invisible. As the cap had to be folded
out of a linen square, with a little practice a girl could
reduce it sufficiently in size so that it stuck attractively on the back of her head. As for the uniform,
a nurse with any feelings of femininity in her veins

immediately took her new outfit to a dressmaker to be shortened.

Shyness and the restrictions surrounding the nurses' social contacts kept me clear of my helpmeets in the ward, apart from the small amount of professional chat I dared to exchange with them. At the same time, the nurses took very little notice of me. With the senior students it was different: for them was the favour of a quick smile behind Sister's back, or a giggle in the sluice-room when no one was in earshot. The house-surgeons, who were doctors and therefore safe matrimonial investments, got cups of coffee when Sister was off duty and had their socks mended; and the registrar could quicken wildly any heart behind a starched apron bodice with a brief smile.

During my stay on Sir Lancelot's firm I began to gain a little confidence in myself in defiance of my surroundings. There was one nurse on the ward who seemed different from the rest. She was a slight little probationer downtrodden by the ward staff as heavily as I, which immediately spun a fine strand of sympathy between us. I felt sorry for her; and I thought, when I was being competently reduced to nothingness by Sister for using Sir Lancelot's special soap at the washbasin, that she was silently commiserating with me.

She was a snub-nosed brunette with grey eyes and a small mouth which she kept firmly closed in the ward. Her experience of St. Swithin's was even less than mine, for she had arrived at the hospital only a fortnight previously. It was aximatic that any nurse who could stand the first six weeks would last the whole course and I was interested to watch her lips growing tighter and tighter as this critical period wore on, while she was discovering it was far less important to save a patient's life than to drop a plate of pudding, and to break a thermometer was a feminine crime just short of persistent shoplifting.

By glances, shy smiles, and putting myself in proximity to her in the ward as much as I dared, I managed to indicate my interest. One morning I was in the sluice-room halfheartedly performing the routine chemical tests on my patients' excreta when she came in and resignedly began to clean out the sink. Sister had sent her there obviously not knowing of my presence; the door shut us off from the ward; we were alone; so I took a chance.

'I say,' I said.

She looked up from the sink.

'I say,' I repeated, 'number six looks much better to-day, doesn't he? The Chief did a good job on him all right. You should have seen the way he got hold of the splenic artery when a clip came off! I've never seen so much blood in my life.'

'Please!' she said, holding her stomach. 'You're making me feel sick.'

'Oh, I'm awfully sorry,' I apologized quickly. 'I just thought you'd be interested.'

'I'm not,' she said. 'The sight of blood makes me sick. In fact, the whole damn place makes me sick. I thought I was going to put my cool hands on the fevered brows of grateful young men, and all I do is clean the floors and give out bedpans to bad-tempered old daddies who smell.'

'If you don't like it,' I suggested, shocked by her confession, 'why did you take it up at all? Why don't you leave?'

'The hell I won't! My mother was a nurse and she's

been ramming it down my throat for nineteen years. If she could take it I damn well can!'

'Would you like to come out to the pictures?' I asked. I thought it best to cut out her complaints and reach my object without further skirmishing. Our privacy might be broken at any moment.

'You bet!' she said without hesitation. 'Anything to get out of this place! I'm off at six. Meet me in the tube station. I must get back to the ward or the old woman will tear me to bits.'

Feeling demurely pleased with myself, I went down to the King George to tell someone about this swift conquest. I found Tony Benskin and Grimsdyke sitting at the bar, energetically talking about racing with the Padre.

'I've just dated up that little pro on the ward,' I told them nonchalantly. 'I'm taking her out to-night.'

Benskin was horrified. He had an obsession that he might one day be trapped into matrimony by a nurse and walked round the hospital as warily as a winning punter passing the men with the three-card trick.

'It's the thin end of the wedge, my boy!' he exclaimed. 'You watch your step, or you'll end up as aisle-fodder before you know where you are. They're vixens, the lot of them.'

'And good luck to them,' Grimsdyke added emphatically. 'After all, that's what they come to the hospital for—to find a husband. They wouldn't admit it, but it's buried in the subconscious of all of them somewhere.'

'I thought nursing was supposed to be a vocation and a calling,' I said defensively.

'No more than our own job, my dear old boy. Why have we all taken up medicine? I've got a good reason, that I'm paid to do it. You've got a doctor as a father and a leaning towards medicine in your case is simply a hereditary defect. Tony here took it up because he couldn't think of anything better that would allow him to play rugger three times a week. How many of our colleagues entered the noble profession through motives of humanity?' Grimsdyke screwed his monocle hard in his eye. 'Damn few, I bet. Humanitarian feelings draw more young fellows annually into the London Fire Brigade. It's the same with the girls—nursing offers one of the few remaining respectable excuses to leave home. Let them marry the chaps, I say. They're strong, healthy girls who know how to cook. To my mind the most important function of the St. Swithin's nursing school is that it provides competent wives to help in general practice anywhere in the world.'

'Three beers please, Padre,' I said, interrupting him. 'Don't you think Grimsdyke's being unfair?'

'You've got to watch your step, sir, you can take it from me,' he said sombrely. 'I've seen more of you young gentlemen caught into marriage when you haven't a ha'penny to your name than I'd like to think about. Children soon, too, sir. Houses, gas bills, vacuum cleaners, and all the other little trappings of matrimony. It's an expensive hobby, take my word, sir, for young fellers before they're settled in practice.'

'Damn it,' I said, 'I've only asked the girl to the pictures. If I don't like her I won't see her again.'

'Easier said than done, sir. Ask Mr. Grimsdyke about that young lady last Christmas.'

Grimsdyke laughed. 'Ah, yes, Padre! I've still got it on me, I think.' He pulled out his wallet and rummaged through the papers it contained. 'Most tiresome woman —tried everything to get rid of her for a fortnight. Then

I received that one morning, handed to me by a hospital porter, if you please.'

He gave me a note in angry feminine handwriting. '*If you do not send an answer to this by midday,*' it said curtly, '*I shall hurl myself off the roof of the Nurses' Home.*'

'What on earth did you say?' I asked, horrified.

'What could I say?' Grimsdyke demanded. 'Except "No reply." '

'Did she throw herself off?'

'I really don't know,' he said, replacing the letter. 'I never troubled to find out.'

I met my little nurse at six. We passed an innocuous evening and arranged a rendezvous for the next week. But the appointment was never kept. The following day she was transferred to Sister Virtue's ward, where she cracked up. One afternoon she threw a pink blancmange at Sister and went out and got a job as a bus conductress.

This incident temporarily cooled my enthusiasm for nurses. After a few weeks I attempted to kindle an affection for a fat blonde girl in the out-patient department, but after we had spent a few evenings together she began to drift away from me, almost imperceptibly at first, like a big ship leaving dock. It was then that I started to worry about myself. Was it that I had no attraction for women? I never enjoyed success with my consorts while my friends apparently had no difficulty in committing fornication with theirs. I slunk into the library and looked up the psychology books: horror overcame me as I turned the pages. In my first few weeks in the wards I had been convinced that I was suffering from such complaints as tuberculosis, rheumatic heart, cancer of the throat, and pernicious anæmia, all of which successfully cleared up in a few days, but now I faced the terrible possibility of harbouring a mother fixation, oral eroticism, and a subnormal libido. I mentioned these fears to my friends that evening after supper.

'The trouble with you, my lad,' said John Bottle, without taking his eye from the microscope he was studying, 'is that you are suffering from that well-recognized clinical condition *orchitis amorosa acuta*, or lover's nuts.'

'Well,' I said sadly, 'I would willingly surrender my virginity if I could find someone to co-operate with me in the matter.'

'Can't you wait for a week?' Kelly asked testily. 'My path. exam is too near to let me go out for a night.'

His objection to my making an immediate start in my love life reflected the most serious menace to harmony in the flat.

We all agreed that it was important we should be able to ask our girl-friends to our home, and with the privacy without which the invitation would be pointless. As accommodation was limited it was equally important that the other three should not be obliged to tramp the streets angrily during the entire evening, or go to bed. Archie and Vera had been no problem because they kept to their own room, but some arrangement had to be made among the rest of us. We decided that each should have one evening a fortnight in which the sitting-room was to be his. A code was arranged: if the girl was brought in and presented to the others it required her host only to mention that it looked like rain for his friends to rise and troop out into the night like a well-drilled squad of infantry. (If he remarked that the weather was turning warmer they did an equally important service by sticking by him.) Then it was up to the man himself. But he had not the entire evening to fritter away in light amours. As the pubs shut at eleven he knew he could only count on the period until then as his own. His comrades would heartlessly return, considering they had left him time enough for a brisk seduction. If he failed to achieve his object in the time, that was his look-out. This probably had bad effects on our psychology, but it made us very persuasive.

'What about that girl from the out-patient department you were taking out?' Tony Benskin asked.

I shrugged my shoulders. 'No good.'

'Won't play?' John Bottle asked with interest. 'I thought as much . . . you want to take my tip and lay off the probationers. Altogether too young and unappreciative. They can still remember the games' mistress said it would ruin their hockey.'

Mike Kelly was sitting in an armchair by the fire, frowning into a yellow-covered book on fevers. He carefully put his finger on his place before speaking.

'You might try the theatre sister from number six,' he suggested faintly.

'Oh, she's no use,' John said with authority. 'Registrars only in that department. She's the sort of girl who'd hardly look at a houseman, let alone a poor bloody student.'

'There's that little blonde staff nurse just come on Loftus's ward,' Mike continued helpfully. 'She looks as if she'd be worth making advances to.'

'Hopeless!' John said. 'She suffers badly from tinnitus—ringing in the ears, and they're wedding bells.'

'How about Rigor Mortis?' Tony suggested, suddenly looking pleased with himself.

'Old Rigor . . . that's more like it!' John agreed. 'She's always ready for a tumble with anybody.'

'The nursery slopes for our friend,' remarked Mike warmly.

'Rigor Mortis?' I asked dubiously.

'Oh, that's not her real name of course,' Tony explained. 'It's Ada something or other. Haven't you come across her?'

'I don't think so.'

'She's not a great beauty,' he went on, 'so perhaps that's why you haven't noticed her. But she has the kindest heart imaginable. She's the staff nurse on Loftus's male ward. I knew her well, old man. I'll introduce you. The more I think of it the more certain I am that she's what you need. She expects the minimum of entertainment and it is hardly necessary to do more than hold her hand and look plaintive. Capital! You shall meet her to-morrow.'

Tony took me to meet Rigor Mortis the following afternoon, when the ward sister was off duty. I immediately agreed that she wasn't much to look at. She had dull black hair which she pushed into her starched cap like the stuffing in a cushion, a chin like a boxer's, and eyebrows that met in the middle.

She was about six feet tall and had a bosom as shapeless as a plate of scrambled eggs. But all these blemishes melted before my eyes, which were fired with Benskin's firm recommendation that she had a kind heart.

After a minute's cheery conversation Tony explained that I had been bursting to make her acquaintance for some months. He asked her if she was doing anything on her next night off; all I had to do was mumble an invitation to the pictures, which she briskly accepted.

I arranged to meet her outside Swan and Edgar's at six and we parted.

'There you are, old man,' Tony said as we left the ward. 'Meet her at six, whip her into a flick, take her back to the flat for a drink—that'll be about nine-thirty. You'll have two solid hours to do your stuff.'

I arranged for the seduction with considerable care. I stayed away from the afternoon lecture and spent the time cleaning up the sitting-room, putting the books away, straightening the cover on the divan, and arranging the reading light so the glow fell romantically in the corner. I set out a new packet of cigarettes and invested in half a bottle of gin. There were two glasses in the kitchen that happened to be the same pattern, and these I carefully washed, dried, and placed on the mantelpiece. It was only five, so I sat down and read the evening paper. I was nervous and worried, as though I was going to the dentist. I began to wish I hadn't introduced the idea at all. But I could no longer back out. I must be victorious by eleven or sink in the opinions of my friends. I took a nip of the gin and set out.

For a few minutes I hoped she wouldn't turn up, but she lumbered out of the Underground right enough. She looked a little better in civilian clothes, but I still thought her as unattractive as an old sofa. I suggested the New Gallery, and she agreed. She seemed fairly friendly, but I soon discovered that she was disinclined to take the initiative in conversation. If I spoke she replied; if I remained silent she appeared to be concentrating heavily on thoughts of her own. I had therefore to keep up a run of inane patter, every sentence on a different subject, until the film released us into merciful mutual silence.

About half-way through the picture I abruptly recalled the object of my expedition. Should I give just the faintest hint of what was to come, I wondered, and hold her hand? It would be the herald's call to the approaching tussle. Would she rebuff this forwardness so early, for I had hardly known her an hour? I gave a sly glance through the darkness and seized her rough palm. She gripped mine without thinking, without an indication that her mind was distracted a hairsbreadth from the screen.

The two of us stood outside in Regent Street. I asked casually if she would care to come home for a drink, and meet the boys. She assented with the same air as she accepted my hand in the cinema. We went to Oxford Circus tube station and I bought a couple of tickets. I held her arm as we walked down the road to the flat and up the steps. The stairs . . . opening the door . . . my surprise that no one was there. She sat down on the divan without a word, and I lit the gas-fire. She took a drink in an off-hand way. We sat in the glow of the gas and the dim light of my romantic bulb.

I finished a cigarette and gave her another drink. Surely, I thought, this would have some effect? She had two or three more, but sat looking absently at the fire, dully returning a sentence for each one of mine, unanimated, unresponsive, unworried.

I nervously looked at my watch and saw with alarm that it was past ten-thirty. I had to get a move on. I felt like a man going out to start an old car on a cold morning.

I held her hand tighter. She didn't object. I drew closer. She moved neither away nor nearer. I put my arm round her and started stroking her off-side ear.

She remained passive, like a cow with its mind on other things.

The seconds ticked away from my wrist, faster and faster. At least, I thought, I have gone this far without rebuff. I kissed her on the cheek. She still sat pleasantly there, saying nothing. Carefully setting down my glass, I stroked her blouse firmly. I might just as well have been brushing her coat. I threw myself at her and she rolled back on the divan like a skittle. With great energy I continued her erotic stimulation. Any moment now, I thought excitedly, and the object of the evening would be achieved. She lay wholly unconcerned. Suddenly she moved. With one hand she picked up the evening paper I had left on the divan. She read the headlines.

'Oh look!' she exclaimed with sympathy, 'there's been an awful train crash at Chelmsford. Seventeen killed!'

*　　*　　*　　*　　*

'So you had no luck?' Tony asked at midnight.

'None. None at all.'

'That's tough. Cheer up . . . . other fish, you know.'

I decided to do my fishing in future in more turbulent waters, even if I had no catch.

9

IN order to teach the students midwifery St. Swithin's supervised the reproductive activities of the few thousand people who lived in the overcrowded area surrounding the hospital. In return, they co-operated by refusing to water down the demands of Nature with the less pressing requests of the Family Planning Association.

The midwifery course is of more value to the student than a piece of instruction on delivering babies. It takes him out of the hospital, where everything is clean and convenient and rolled up on sterile trollies, to the environment he will be working in when he goes into practice—a place of dirty floors, bed-bugs, no hot water, and lights in the most inconvenient places; somewhere without nurses but with bands of inquisitive children and morbid relatives; a world of broken stairs, unfindable addresses, and cups of tea in the kitchen afterwards.

It was fortunate that I was plunged into the practice of midwifery shortly after my unfruitful love life, for it is a subject which usually produces a sharp reactionary attack of misogyny in its students. Tony Benskin, Grimsdyke, and myself started 'on the district' together. We had to live in the hospital while we were midwifery clerks, in rooms the size of isolation cubicles on the top floor of the resident doctors' quarters. My predecessor, a tall, fair-haired, romantic-looking man called Lamont had been so moved by his experiences he was on the point of beaking off his engagement.

'The frightful women!' he said heatedly, as he tried to cram a pile of text-books into his case. 'I can't understand that anyone would ever want to sleep with them. That someone obviously has done so in the near past is quite beyond me.'

'How many babies have you had?' I asked.

'Forty-nine. That includes a couple of Cæsars. I'd have made a half-century if I hadn't missed a B.B.A.'

'B.B.A.?'

'Born before arrival. Terrible disgrace for the midder clerk, of course. I reckoned I'd have time for my lunch first, and when I got there the blasted thing was in the bed. However, mother and child did well, so I suppose no real harm was done. Don't try and open the window, it's stuck. I'm going out to get drunk. Best of luck.'

Picking up his bag he left, the latest penitent for the sin of Adam.

I sat on the bed, feeling depressed. It was an unusually raw afternoon in November and the sky hung over the roof-tops in an unbroken dirty grey sheet. There was no fire in the room and the pipes emitted flatulent noises but no heat. The only decoration was a large black-and-white map of the district on which some former student had helpfully added the pubs in red ink. I looked out of the window and saw a few flakes of snow—ominous, like the first spots of a smallpox rash. I wished women would go away and bud, like the flowers.

The three of us reported to the senior resident

obstetrical officer, a worried-looking young man whom we found in the ante-natal clinic. This clinic was part of the St. Swithin's service. Every Thursday afternoon the mothers came and sat on the benches outside the clinic door, looking like rows of over-ripe poppy-heads. The obstetrical officer was absently running his hands over an abdomen like the dome of St. Paul's to find which way up the baby was.

'You the new clerks?' he asked, without interest.

We each nodded modestly.

'Well, make sure you're always within call. When you go out on a case a midwife will be sent separately by the local maternity service, so you've got nothing to worry about. Don't forget to carry two pennies in your pocket.

'To 'phone, of course,' he said when I asked why. 'If you get into trouble dash for the nearest box and call me, and I'll come out in a police car. Don't wait till it's too late, either.'

He dismissed us and bent over to listen to the fœtal heart rate with a stethoscope shaped like a small flower-vase.

Our next call was on the Extern Sister, who controlled all the midwifery students. I found her a most interesting woman. She was so ugly she could never have had much expectation of fulfilling her normal biological function; now she had been overtaken by the sad menopause and was left no chance of doing so at all. As she had not been offered the opportunity of bearing children she had thrown herself into midwifery like a novice into religion. She knew more about it than the obstetrical officer. She could talk only about mothers and babies and thought of everyone solely as a reproductive element. In her room was a gold medal she had won in her examinations, which she proudly displayed in a small glass-covered frame between two prints of Peter Scott's ducks. She talked of the anatomy involved in the birth of a baby as other women described their favourite shopping street. She had, however, the unfortunate trick of awarding the parts of the birth canal to the listener.

'When your cervix is fully dilated,' she told us gravely, 'you must decide whether to apply your forceps to your baby. You must feel to see if your head or your breech is presenting.'

'Supposing it's your shoulder or your left ear?' asked Benskin.

'Then you put your hand in your uterus and rotate your child,' she replied without hesitation.

She gave us a rough idea of delivering babies and demonstrated the two instrument bags we had to take on our cases. They were long leather affairs, like the luggage of a dressy cricketer, containing sufficient material to restore the biggest disaster it was likely a student could pull down on himself. There were bottles of antiseptic, ether and chloroform, needles and catgut in tins of Lysol, a pair of obstetrical forceps, a peculiar folding canvas arrangement for holding up the mother's legs, enamel bowls, rubber gloves, and a number of unidentifiable packages.

'You must check your bags before you go to your mother,' Sister said.

We chalked our room-numbers on the board in the hall and went out for a drink in the King George. The snow was falling thickly, swirling round the lamp-posts and clinging to the hospital walls, giving the old building a more sinister appearance than ever.

'What a night to start stork-chasing!' Grimsdyke exclaimed.

'What happens when we get out there?' I asked.

'Getting nervous, old boy?'

'I am a bit. I haven't seen a baby born before. I might faint or something.'

'There's nothing to worry about,' Benskin told me cheerfully. 'I was talking to one of the chaps we're relieving. The midwife always gets there first and tells you what to do under her breath. They're a good crowd. They let the patient think you're the doctor, which is good for the morale of both of you.'

We went back to the hospital for dinner. Afterwards Benskin asked the duty porter if everything was still quiet.

'Not a thing, sir,' he replied. 'It's a bad sign, all right. After it's been as quiet as this for a bit they start popping out like rabbits from their warrens.'

We sat in Grimsdyke's room and played poker for matches for a couple of hours. It was difficult to concentrate on the game. Every time the 'phone bell rang in the distance we jumped up nervously together. Grimsdyke suggested bed at ten, predicting we would be roused as soon as we dropped off to sleep. We cut for who should be on first call: I lost.

It was four when the porter woke me up. He cheerily pulled off the bedclothes and handed me a slip of paper with an address scribbled on it in pencil.

'You'd better hurry, sir,' he said. 'They sounded proper worried over the 'phone.'

I rolled out of bed and dressed with the enthusiasm of a prisoner on his execution morning. The night outside was as thick and white as a rice pudding. After a glance through the curtains I pulled a green-and-yellow hooped rugby jersey over my shirt and a dirty cricket sweater over that. I tucked the ends of my trousers into football stockings, wrapped a long woollen scarf round my neck and hid the lot under a duffle coat. I looked as if I was going to take the middle watch on an Arctic fishing vessel.

The reason for this conscientious protection against the weather was the form of transport allotted to the students to reach their cases. It was obviously impossible to provide such inconsequential people with a car and we were nearly all too poor to own one ourselves. On the other hand, if the students had been forced to walk to their patients the race would have gone to the storks. A compromise had therefore been effected some ten years ago and the young obstetricians had the loan of the midwifery bicycle.

This vehicle had unfortunately not worn well in the service of the obstetrical department. It had originally been equipped with such necessaries as brakes, mud-guards, lights, and rubber blocks on the pedals, but, as human beings sadly lose their hair, teeth, and firm subcutaneous fat in the degeneration of age, the machine had similarly been reduced to its bare comfortless bones. The saddle had the trick of slipping unexpectedly and throwing the rider either backwards or forwards, it was impossible to anticipate. The only way to stop the machine was by falling off. It was the most dangerous complication of midwifery in the practice of the hospital.

I searched for the address on the map. It was on the other side of the district, a short, narrow, coy street hiding between a brewery and a goods yard. It seemed as remote as Peru.

I waddled down to the out-patient hall to collect the

instrument bags. The place was cold and deserted; the porter who had called me was yawning in the corner over the telephone, and the two night nurses huddled in their cloaks round their tiny electric fire, sewing their way through a stack of gauze dressings. They took no notice of the globular figure coming down the stairs: an insignificant midwifery clerk wasn't worth dropping a stitch for. For the houseman, or, if they were lucky, one of the registrars come to open an emergency appendix—to them they would give a cup of coffee and a flutter of the eyelids. But what good were the junior students?

The bicycle was kept in a small shed in the hospital courtyard, and had for its stablemate the long trolley used for moving unlucky patients to the mortuary. I saw that the first problem of the case was balancing myself and my equipment on the machine. As well as the two leather bags I had a couple of drums the size of biscuit barrels containing the sterilized dressings. There was a piece of thick string attached to the bicycle, which I felt was probably part of its structure, but I removed it and suspended the two drums round my neck like a yoke. Carefully mounting the machine, I clung to the bags and the handlebars with both hands and pedalled uncertainly towards the front gate. The snowflakes fell upon me eagerly, like a crowd of mosquitoes, leaping for my face, the back of my neck, and my ankles.

The few yards across the courtyard were far enough to indicate the back tyre was flat and the direction of the front wheel had no constant relationship to the way the handlebars were pointing. I crunched to a stop by the closed iron gates and waited for the porter to leave his cosy cabin and let me out.

'You all right, sir?' he asked with anxiety.

'Fine,' I said, 'I love it like this. It makes me feel like a real doctor.'

'Well,' he said dubiously, 'good luck, sir.'

'Thank you.'

The porter turned the key in the lock and pulled one of the gates open against the resisting snow.

'Your back light isn't working, sir,' he shouted.

I called back I thought it didn't matter and pedalled away into the thick night feeling like Captain Oates. I had gone about twenty yards when the chain came off.

After replacing the chain I managed to wobble along the main road leading away from the hospital in the direction of the brewery. The buildings looked as hostile as polar ice-cliffs. Everything appeared so different from the kindly daytime, which gave life to the cold, dead streets with the brisk circulation of traffic. Fortunately my thorough knowledge of the local public houses provided a few finger-posts, and I might have done tolerably well as a flying angel of mercy if the front wheel hadn't dropped off.

I fell into the snow in the gutter and wished I had gone in for the law. As I got to my feet I reflected that the piece of string might have been something important to do with the attachment of the front wheel; but now the lesion was inoperable. Picking up my luggage, I left the machine to be covered by the snow like a dead husky and trudged on. By now I was fighting mad. I told myself I would damn well deliver that baby. If it dared to precipitate itself into the world ungraciously without waiting for me I decided I would strangle it.

I turned off the main road towards the brewery, but

after a few hundred yards I had to admit I was lost.
Even the pubs were unfamiliar. I now offered no
resistance to my environment and submissively felt the
moisture seeping through my shoes. I leant against a
sheltering doorpost, preparing to meet death in as
gentlemanly a way as possible.

At that moment a police car, forced like myself into
the snow, stopped in front of me. The driver swung his
light on my load and on myself, and had no alternative
than to decide I was a suspicious character. He asked
for my identity card.

'Quick!' I said dramatically. 'I am going to a woman
in childbirth.'

'Swithin's?' asked the policeman.

'Yes. It may be too late. I am the doctor.'

'Hop in the back!'

There is nothing that delights policemen more than
being thrown into a midwifery case. There is a chance
they might have to assist in the performance, which
means a picture in the evening papers and congratula-
tory beer in the local. The constable who walked into
St. Swithin's one afternoon with an infant born on
the lower deck of a trolley bus looked as pleased as if he
were the father.

The warm police car took me to the address, and the
crew abandoned me with reluctance. It was a tall,
dead-looking tenement for ever saturated with the
smells of brewing and shunting. I banged on the
knocker and waited.

A thin female child of about five opened the door.

'I'm the doctor,' I announced.

The arrival of the obstetrician in such a briskly
multiplying area caused no more stir than the visit of
the milkman.

'Upstairs, mate,' she said and scuttled away into the darkness like a rat.

The house breathed the sweet stench of bed-bugs; inside it was dark, wet, and rotting. I fumbled my way to the stairs and creaked upwards. On the second floor a door opened a foot, a face peered through, and as the shaft of light caught me it was slammed shut. It was on the fifth and top floor that the accouchement seemed to be taking place, as there was noise and light coming from under one of the doors. I pushed it open and lumbered in.

'Don't worry!' I said. 'I have come.'

I took a look round the room. It wasn't small, but a lot was going on in it. In the centre, three or four children were fighting on the pockmarked linoleum for possession of their plaything, a piece of boxwood with a nail through it. A fat woman was unconcernedly making a cup of tea on a gas-ring in one corner, and in the other a girl of about seventeen with long yellow hair was reading last Sunday's *News of the World*. A cat, sympathetic to the excited atmosphere, leapt hysterically among the children. Behind the door was a bed beside which was grandma—who always appears on these occasions, irrespective of the social standing of the participants. Grandma was giving encouragement tempered with warning to the mother, a thin, pale, fragile woman on the bed, and it was obvious that the affair had advanced alarmingly. A tightly-packed fire roared in the grate and above the mantelpiece Field-Marshal Montgomery, of all people, looked at the scene quizzically.

'Her time is near, doctor,' said grandma with satisfaction.

'You have no need to worry any longer, missus,' I said brightly.

I dropped the kit on the floor and removed my duffle coat, which wept dirty streams on to the lino. The first step was to get elbow room and clear out the non-playing members of the team.

'Who are you?' I asked the woman making tea.

'From next door,' she replied. 'I thought she'd like a cup of tea, poor thing.'

'I want some hot water,' I said sternly. 'Lots of hot water. Fill basins with it. Or anything you like. Now you all go off and make me some hot water. Take the children as well. Isn't it past their bedtime?'

'They sleep in 'ere, doctor,' said grandma.

'Oh. Well—they can give you a hand. And take the cat with you. Come on—all of you. Lots of water, now.'

They left unwillingly, in disappointment. They liked their entertainment to be fundamental.

'Now, mother,' I started, when we were alone. A thought struck me—hard, in the pit of the stomach. The midwife—the cool, practised, confident midwife. Where was she? To-night—this memorable night to the two of us in the room—what had happened to her? Snowbound, of course. I felt like an actor who had forgotten his lines and finds the prompter has gone out for a drink.

'Mother,' I said earnestly. 'How many children have you?'

'Five, doctor,' she groaned.

Well, that was something. At least one of us knew a bit about it.

She began a frightening increase in activity.

'I think it's coming, doctor!' she gasped, between pains. I grasped her hand vigorously.

'You'll be right as rain in a minute,' I said, as confidently as possible. 'Leave it to me.'

'I feel sick,' she cried miserably.

'So do I,' I said.

I wondered what on earth I was going to do.

There was, however, one standby that I had thought-fully taken the trouble to carry. I turned into the corner furthest away from the mother and looked as if I was waiting confidently for the precise time to intervene. Out of my hip pocket I drew a small but valuable volume in a limp red cover—*The Student's Friend in Obstetrical Difficulties*. It was written by a hard-headed obstetrician on the staff of a Scottish hospital who was under no illusions about what the students would find difficult. It started off with 'The Normal Delivery.' The text was written without argument, directly, in short numbered paragraphs, like a cookery book. I glanced at the first page.

'Sterility,' it said. 'The student must try to achieve sterile surroundings for the delivery, and scrub-up him-self as for a surgical operation. Newspapers may be used if sterile towels are unobtainable, as they are often bacteria-free.'

Newspaper, that was it! There was a pile of them in the corner, and I scattered the sheets over the floor and the bed. This was a common practice in the district, and if he knew how many babies were born yearly straight on to the *Daily Herald* Mr. Percy Cudlip would be most surprised.

There was a knock on the door, and grandma passed through an enamel bowl of boiling water.

'Is it come yet, doctor?' she asked.

'Almost,' I told her. 'I shall need lots more water.'

I put the bowl down on the table, took some soap and a brush from the bag, and started scrubbing.

'Oh, doctor, doctor . . .!' cried the mother.

'Don't get alarmed,' I said airily.

'It's coming, doctor!'

I scrubbed furiously. The mother groaned. Grandma shouted through the door she had more hot water. I shouted back at her to keep out. The cat, which had not been removed as ordered, jumped in the middle of the newspaper and started tearing at it with its claws.

Suddenly I became aware of a new note in the mother's cries—a higher, wailing, muffled squeal. I dropped the soap and tore back the bedclothes.

*　　*　　*　　*　　*

The baby was washed and tucked up in one of the drawers from the wardrobe, which did a turn of duty as a cot about once a year. The mother was delighted and said she had never had such a comfortable delivery. The spectators were readmitted, and cooed over the infant. There were cups of tea all round. I had the best one, with sugar in it. I felt the name of the medical profession never stood higher.

'Do you do a lot of babies, doctor?' asked the mother.

'Hundreds,' I said. 'Every day.'

'What's your name, doctor, if you don't mind?' she said. I told her.

'I'll call 'im after you. I always call them after the doctor or the nurse, according.'

I beamed and bowed graciously. I was genuinely proud of the child. It was my first baby, born through my own skill and care. I had already forgotten in the flattering atmosphere that my single manœuvre in effecting the delivery was pulling back the eiderdown.

Packing the instruments up, I climbed into my soggy duffle coat and, all smiles, withdrew. At the front door I found to my contentment that the snow had stopped and the roads shone attractively in the lamplight. I began to whistle as I walked away. At that moment the midwife turned the corner on her bicycle.

'Sorry, old chap,' she said, as she drew up. 'I was snowed under. Have you been in?'

'In! It's all over.'

'Did you have any trouble?' she asked dubiously.

'Trouble!' I said with contempt. 'Not a bit of it! It went splendidly.'

'I suppose you remembered to remove the after-birth?'

'Of course.'

'Well, I might as well go home then. How much did it weigh?'

'Nine pounds on the kitchen scales.'

'You students are terrible liars.'

I walked back to the hospital over the slush as if it were a thick pile carpet. The time was getting on. A hot bath, I thought, then a good breakfast . . . and a day's work already behind me. I glowed in anticipation as I suddenly became aware that I was extremely hungry.

At the hospital gate the porter jumped up from his seat.

' 'Urry up, sir,' he said, 'and you'll just make it.'

'What's all this?' I asked with alarm.

'Another case, sir. Been waiting two hours. The other gentlemen are out already.'

'But what about my breakfast?'

'Sorry, sir. Not allowed to go to meals if there's a case. Orders of the Dean.'

'Oh, hell!' I said. I took the grubby slip of paper bearing another address. 'So this is midwifery,' I added gloomily.

'That's right, sir,' said the porter cheerfully. 'It gets 'em all down in the end.'

10

EVERYONE working in hospital is so preoccupied with the day-to-day rush of minor crises that the approach of Christmas through the long, dark, bronchitic weeks of midwinter comes as a surprise. The holiday cuts brightly into hospital routine, like an unexpected ray of sunlight in an Inner Circle tunnel. At St. Swithin's there was, however, one prodromal sign of the approaching season—a brisk increase in attendance at the children's department.

Every year at Christmas the Governors gave a tea-party in the main hall of the hospital for a thousand or so of the local boys and girls. They were men not used to stinting their hospitality, and provided richly for the tastes of their guests. It was the sort of affair that could be adequately described only by Ernest Hemingway, Negley Farson, or some other writer with a gift of extracting a forceful attractiveness from descriptions of active animals feeding in large numbers.

The children began to collect outside the locked doors of the out-patient department soon after midday; by three the front of the hospital looked like an Odeon on Saturday morning. At four sharp the doors were opened by the porters and the mob were funnelled into the building—scratching, fighting, shouting, and screaming, their incidental distractions from the fists and elbows of their neighbours overwhelmed with the urgent common desire to get at the food. They rushed through the entrance lobby, stormed the broad, wooden-floored hall, and expended their momentum in a pile of sticky, white-glazed buns.

The buns were the foundation of the party, but there was a great deal more besides—a high Christmas cake flaming with candles, churns of strawberry ice-cream, jellies the colours of traffic lights, oranges with a tenacious aroma, and sweet tea in long enamelled jugs. The non-edible attractions included paper chains, crackers, funny hats, a tree ten feet high, and Father Christmas. It was the duty of the children's house-physician to play this part. The gown, whiskers, sack, and toys were provided by the Governors; all the doctor had to do was allow himself to be lowered in a fire-escape apparatus from the roof into the tight mob of children screaming below. This obligation he discharged with the feelings of a nervous martyr being dropped into the bear-pit.

It was inevitable that he should breathe heavily on his little patients a strong smell of mixed liquors, which never missed their sharp, experienced noses and gave rise to delighted comments:

'Coo! 'Ees bin boozing!'

'Smells like Dad on Saturday!'

'Give us a train, Mister!'

All this the house-physician had to endure with a set smile of determined benevolence.

The party was controlled, where possible, by the out-patient sister and a reinforced staff of nurses. Their starched caps and aprons melted in the afternoon with the ice-cream as they attempted to impose the principle of fair shares on a community demonstrating a vigorous capitalist spirit of grabbing what they could. The energy of the children diminished only if they had to retire to a corner to be sick; but the hospitality of St. Swithin's was unlimited, and it usually happened that several of the little guests were later asked to stay the night.

The reason that the annual tea-party afforded as sure an indication that Christmas was approaching as a polite postman lay in the rules for admission to the jamboree. The Governors had decided many years ago that as it was impossible to entertain every child in the district invitations should be sent only to those who had attended the hospital in the months of November and December. As all the children within several miles knew of the party and were perfectly familiar with the qualifications for entry the increase in juvenile morbidity after October 31st was always alarming. This had recently led an ingenuous new house-physician in the department to sit down and prepare for publication in the *Lancet* a scientific paper on the startling increase in stomach-ache and growing pains among London school children in the last quarter of the year.

The goings-on at Christmas-time were conducted with the excuse that the staff was obliged to entertain the patients, just as adults take themselves off to circuses and pantomimes on the pretext of amusing the children. The wards were decorated, the out-patient hall spanned with streamers, and on Christmas Day even the operating theatres were festooned. The hospital presented the grotesque appearance of a warship during Navy Week, when the guns and other sinister implements aboard are covered with happy bunting. Relatives, friends, visiting staff, old graduates, and students overran the place; it was an enormous family party.

I had dutifully returned home the first Christmas I was in the hospital, but for the second I decided to stay and join in the fun. I was then coming to the end of my second session of medical clerking, this time as a protégé of the Dean, Dr. Loftus, on Prudence ward.

A week before Christmas Eve the ward sister distributed sheets of coloured crêpe paper round the patients and set them cutting frilly shades for the bed-lamps, paper chains, cut-outs for sticking on the windows, and the other paraphernalia of Christmas. Sister Prudence was different from the majority of her colleagues at St. Swithin's. She was a fat, kindly, jovial woman with an inefficiently concealed affection for Guinness' stout. She never had a bitter word for the students, whom she regarded as pleasantly irresponsible imbeciles, and she treated the nurses as normally fallible human beings. Above all, she had the superb recommendation of hating Sister Virtue's guts.

'I'm so worried about number twelve,' she said to me quietly one afternoon. I followed her glance to a wizened, sallow old man lying flat on his back cutting out a red paper doll with no enthusiasm. 'I do hope he won't die before Christmas,' she continued. 'It would be such a pity for him to miss it all!'

On Christmas Eve the students and nurses tacked up the paper chains and fixed the Christmas tree in front of the sanitary-looking door of the sluice-room. Sister beamed at the volunteers, as she was by then certain her ward would be more richly decorated than Sister Virtue's. It was a vivid jungle in paper. Red and yellow streamers hung in shallow loops across the forbidding ceiling and the dark woodwork of the walls was covered refreshingly with coloured stars, circles, and rosettes, like a dull winter flower-bed in springtime. The severely

functional lights over the beds were softened by paper
lanterns, which emitted so little light, however, that
they transformed even a simple manœuvre like giving
an injection into an uncomfortable and dangerous
operation. The black iron bedrails were garlanded with
crimson crêpe, the long table down the middle of the
ward was banked with synthetic snow, and blatantly
unsterile holly flourished unrebuked in every corner.
Most important of all, a twig of mistletoe hung over the
doorway. By hospital custom, to avoid interruption in
the daily working of the ward the sprig was not put into
use until Christmas morning; before then the nurses
and the students took a new and keen appraisal of each
other with sidelong glances, each deciding whom they
would find themselves next to when the sport opened.
As for Sister Prudence, she would have taken it as a
personal insult not to be embraced by everyone from
Dr. Loftus down to the most junior student. 'I *do* like
Christmas!' she said enthusiastically. 'It's the only time
an old body like me ever gets kissed!'

The students had a more exacting task at Christmas
than simply decorating the ward. It was a tradition at
St. Swithin's that each firm produced, and presented in
one of the main wards, a short theatrical entertainment.
This was in accordance with the established English
custom of dropping the national mantle of self-consciousness at Christmas-time and revealing the horrible
likeness of the charade underneath. No one at St.
Swithin's would have shirked acting in, or witnessing,
the Christmas shows any more than they would have
contemplated refusing to operate on an acute appendix.
They were part of the hospital history, and it was
handed down that Sir Benjamin Bone himself when a
student contributed a fine baritone to the Christmas

entertainment while the young Larrymore accompanied him on a violin, deliberately out of key.

The dramatic construction of these performances was as rigidly conventional as classical Greek drama or provincial pantomime. There were certain things that had to be included, or the audience was left wondering and cheated. It was essential at one point for a large student to appear dressed as a nurse, with two pairs of rugger socks as falsies. There had to be a song containing broad references to the little professional and personal idiosyncrasies of the consultant staff—oddities that they had previously been under the impression passed unnoticed. Equally important were unsubtle jests about bedpans and similar pieces of hospital furniture. One scene had to represent a patient suffering under the attentions of a scrum of doctors and students, and there was always a burst of jolly community singing at the end.

The players had their conventions as well. No troupe would have contemplated for a moment taking the boards sober, and the most important member of the cast was the supernumerary who wheeled round the firkin of beer on a stretcher. It was also essential to carry a spare actor or two in the company, as on most occasions some of the active performers were overcome before the last scenes and had to be carried to the wings.

Two days before Christmas Grimsdyke took the initiative by ordering our firm to assemble in the King George at opening time that evening. There were seven of us: Grimsdyke and Tony Benskin, John Bottle, the middle-aged student Sprogget, Evans, the brilliant Welshman, the keen student Harris, and myself. We collected round the piano in a corner of the bar.

'Now, look here, you fellows,' Grimsdyke began with authority. 'We must scratch up a bit of talent between us. Time's getting short. We've only got a day and a half to write, produce, and rehearse what will be the most magnificent of performances that ever hit St. Swithin's. Can any of you chaps play the piano?'

'I can play a bit,' I said. 'But mostly hymns.'

'That doesn't matter. Those hymn tunes can be turned into anything you like with a bit of ingenuity. That's one thing settled at any rate. What sort of piece shall we do? A panto, or a sort of pierrot show?'

'I think I ought to tell you,' said Harris aggressively, 'that I am considered pretty hot stuff at singing Little Polly Perkins from Paddington Green. I gave it at the church concert at home last year and it made quite a sensation.'

'Please!' said Grimsdyke. 'Can anyone else do anything? You can conjure, can't you, Tony?'

'One does the odd trick,' Benskin admitted modestly. 'Nothing spectacular like sawing a nurse in half, though—just rabbits out of hats and suchlike.'

'It'll amuse the kids, so we'll put you in. You can also dress up as a nurse somewhere in the show. John, you'd better take the romantic lead. What can you do, Sprogget?'

'Me? Oh, well, I don't do anything . . . that is, well, you know . . .' He gave an embarrassed giggle. 'I do child imitations.'

'Good for you. Child imitations it shall be. Evans, my dear old boy, you shall be general understudy, stage manager, wardrobe mistress, and ale carrier. You haven't got one of those lilting Welsh voices, I suppose?'

'My voice is only any good when diluted with forty thousand others at Twickenham.'

'Oh well, Harris will have to sing, I suppose. It's unavoidable. That seems to have settled the casting difficulties.'

'What about you? What are you going to do?' I asked him.

'I shall write, produce, and compère the piece, as well as reciting a short poem of my own composition in honour of St. Swithin's. I think it should go over very well. I suppose nobody has any objections to that?'

We shook our heads submissively.

'Good. Now what we want is a title. It must be short, snappy, brilliantly funny, and with a medical flavour the patients can understand. Any suggestions?'

The seven of us thought for a few minutes in silence.

'How about "Laughing Gas"?' I suggested.

Grimsdyke shook his head. 'Too trite.'

' "Babies in the Ward "?' said Benskin eagerly. 'Or "The Ninety-niners"?'

'They were both used last year.'

'I've got it!' Harris jumped up from behind the piano.
' "Enema for the Skylark"! How's that?'

'Horrible.'

We thought again. Grimsdyke suddenly snapped his fingers. 'Just the thing!' he announced. 'The very thing! What's wrong with "Jest Trouble"?'

His cast looked at him blankly.

' "Jest trouble," you see,' he explained. 'Pun on "Chest Trouble." All the patients know what that means. Get it? Exactly the right touch, I think. Now let's get on and write a script.'

The production was born with—in relation to its small size and immaturity—intense labour pains. As the cast had to continue their routine hospital work the producer found it difficult to assemble them on one spot at the same time; and when they did arrive, each one insisted on rewriting the script as he went along. I drooped over the piano trying hard to transform the melody of 'Onward Christian Soldiers' into a suitable accompaniment for a cautionary duet Benskin and Grimsdyke insisted on singing, beginning:

> *'If the ill that troubles you is a tendency to lues,*
> *And you're positive your Wasserman is too.'*

And ending:

> *'My poor little baby, he's deaf and he's dumb,*
> *My poor little baby's insane:*
> *He's nasty big blisters all over his tum,*
> *What a shame, what a shame, what a shame!'*

When the King George closed we moved to the deserted students' common room; when we were hoarse and exhausted we flopped to sleep on the springless sofas. We rehearsed grimly all the next day. Late on Christmas Eve Grimsdyke rubbed his hands and announced: 'This would bring a smile to the lips of a chronic melancholic.'

11

THE patients saw plenty of Christmas Day. They were woken up by the night nurses at five a.m. as usual, given a bowl of cold water, and wished a Merry Christmas. After breakfast the nurses took off their uniform caps and put on funny hats, and shifted into hidden side-wards any patients who seemed likely to spoil the fun by inconsiderately passing away. Sister Virtue was particularly successful in the rôle of Valkyrie: her long experience of diseases and doctors enabled her to spot a declining case several days before the medical staff. She had only to fix her glare on an apparently convalescent patient and give her bleak opinion that 'He won't *do*, sir,' and the houseman confidently made arrangements for the post-mortem.

When I arrived on the ward in the middle of the morning I found a wonderful end-of-term spirit abroad. People were allowed to do things they felt forbidden even to contemplate at any other time in the year. Smoking was permitted all day, not only in the regulation hour after meals, the radio was turned on before noon, and, as if this wasn't enough, the patients were issued with a bottle of beer apiece.

Sister was visiting each of the beds distributing presents from the tree, and two up-patients, dressing-gowned old gentlemen with a brace of alarming blood pressures, were dancing the highland fling in nurses' caps and aprons. Three or four of the students were steadfastly pursuing nurses with sprigs of mistletoe: the chase was not exacting.

As I entered the ward a giggling nurse ran out of the sluice-room followed by Tony Benskin, who had a look of intense eagerness on his face.

'That's enough, Mr. Benskin!' she cried. 'You've had enough!'

Benskin pulled up as he caught sight of me.

'I thought you said you were coming early to test urine,' I remarked.

'One meets one's friends,' he explained simply. 'One must be social. After all, it's Christmas. Come in the sluice-room. I've got a bottle.'

I followed him in.

'And I thought you were scared of nurses.'

'Delightful creatures,' said Benskin, beaming. 'So refreshingly sex-starved.'

I noticed the gin bottle he had invited me to.

'Good God, Tony,' I said. 'Have you got through all that so early in the day?'

'It's Christmas, old boy.'

'Tony, you're sloshed already.'

'What of it? There's plenty more gin in the instrument cupboard. Grimsdyke hid it there yesterday. After all, it's Christmas. Have a drink.'

'All right. I suppose it's my party as much as yours.'

The gin in the instrument cupboard was finished by midday, when Dr. Lionel Loftus appeared with his wife, and his two ugly daughters that were produced every Christmas-time like the decorations but without success. He got a hilarious reception.

'Here's the old Dean!' cried Benskin, leaping up on a bed. 'Three cheers for the Dean, boys! Three cheers for old Lofty! Three cheers for the jolly old Dean!'

The Dean stood, all smiles, in the doorway, while three cheers were given and the ward broke into 'For He's a Jolly Good Fellow.' He kissed Sister under the mistletoe, presented his housemen with a bottle of sherry, and shook hands with the patients. His own part in the programme was fairly simple: all he had to do was put on a chef's hat and carve the turkey in the middle of the ward. He was not good at carving and the last patients had a cold meal, which was the disadvantage of eating Christmas dinner on the medical side of the hospital. The surgeons were naturally more skilful, and Sir Lancelot Spratt had been known to slit a bird to ribbons in a couple of minutes.

During dinner Grimsdyke appeared. I was sitting on a bed with my arm round a nurse. Both of us were blowing squeakers.

'Hello, old boy,' Grimsdyke said in a worried tone. 'Merry Christmas and all that sort of thing. How are you feeling?'

'Fine! Have a drink.'

'All the boys are pretty high, I suppose?'

'Of course. Benskin's as stiff as a plank.'

'Oh God! I hope he'll be all right to go on this afternoon.'

I put my squeaker down contritely.

'I'd clean forgotten about that! Perhaps we'd better go and see how he is.'

'Where's he got to?' Grimsdyke asked nervously.

The nurse told him. 'I saw him going into the sluice-room. He said he felt tired and wanted a rest.'

Benskin was resting when we found him. He was

lying on the stone floor with his head against the base of the sink.

'Wake up! Wake up!' Grimsdyke commanded, with an anxious note in his voice. 'The show, man! We're due to start in half an hour!'

Benskin grunted.

'Oh Lord!' Grimsdyke said in despair. 'We'll never get him on the stage. . . . Tony! Benskin! Pull yourself together!'

Benskin opened his eyes fleetingly.

'Merry Christmas,' he muttered.

'Why not try an ice-pack on his head?' I suggested. 'Or an intravenous injection of vitamin C? It's supposed to oxidize the alcohol.'

'We'll try throwing water over him. It might be some use. Give me that measuring glass.'

We poured a pint of cold water over the ineffective actor; he lay dripping like a cherub on a fountain, but equally inactive.

'Let's hold him by the arms and legs and shake him,' I said.

'Do you think it would do any good?'

'It may do. Shock therapy is sometimes effective.'

Grimsdyke held Benskin's arms, and I took his feet. He was a heavy man, and we strained as we lifted him.

'Ready?' Grimsdyke asked. 'Right—one, two, three, shake.'

We were still shaking when the sluice-room door opened and Sister Prudence walked in.

'Hello!' she said. 'What's up?'

'Mr. Benskin fainted,' Grimsdyke said quickly. 'I think the excitement was too much for him.'

Sister Prudence shot a diagnostic look at the patient.

Her professional training enabled her to act swiftly and decisively when faced with an emergency.

'Nurse!' she called, starting to roll up her sleeves. 'Run down to the accident department and bring up the suicide box. Take your jacket off, Mr. Grimsdyke. You can help me with the stomach pump.'

*　　*　　*　　*　　*

Benskin's stomach was washed out with bicarbonate solution, which was always kept handy to frustrate local suicides. He was given a cup of black coffee and a benzedrine tablet. By that time he maintained that he was ready to face his audience.

'It will be a pallid performance,' he admitted thickly. 'But at least I shall be on my feet.'

The show was due to open in Fortitude ward, on the male surgical side.

'Always test on men's surgical,' Grimsdyke said. 'Surgical patients are either well or dead. They don't hang about in the miserable twilight like medical ones. Besides, half the medical patients have got gastric ulcers, and who can feel jolly on Christmas Day after a poached egg and a glass of milk?'

Our troupe arrived made-up and in the costume of white flannels and shirts with green bow ties that Grimsdyke had ordered. The stage was improvised on the floor at one end of the ward out of the screens otherwise used to hide patients from their companions. Grimsdyke, who succeeded in looking smart in his flannels, worried his way round his indifferent actors like the headmistress at a kindergarten play.

'Are we ready to start?' he asked anxiously. 'Where's the piano?'

'It looks as if we've lost it somewhere,' I told him.

'It doesn't matter about the bloody piano,' John Bottle cut in. 'We've lost the beer as well.'

Grimsdyke and Bottle disappeared to find these two essential articles of stage furniture, while Harris muttered the words of Polly Perkins over to himself repeatedly, Sprogget stood in the corner with a look of painful concentration on his face talking like a three-year-old girl, and I rubbed red grease-paint into Benskin's white cheeks.

'What are you feeling like now?' I asked him.

'I often wondered what it was like to be dead,' he said. 'Now I know. Still, the show must go on. One cannot disappoint one's public.'

The piano, the actors, and the beer were collected on the same spot; the audience, who had been waiting uncomfortably on the floor, on the edge of beds, or leaning against the wall began a burst of impatient clapping.

'For God's sake!' said Grimsdyke frantically. 'Let's get going. Are you ready, Richard? What the hell are you doing underneath the piano?'

'I seem to have lost the music for the opening chorus,' I explained.

'Play any damn thing you like. Play the closing chorus. Play God Save the King.'

'I'll vamp.'

The screen representing the proscenium curtain was pushed aside, and the only presentation of Jest Trouble took the boards.

The performance was not a great success. It happened that Mr. Hubert Cambridge, the surgeon in charge of Fortitude ward, had a desire to remove two hundred stomachs during the year and had approached Christmas in a flurry of gastrectomies. As the patients

had not a whole stomach between them and each had
suffered a high abdominal incision that made even
breathing painful they were not a responsive and easy-
laughing audience. The nurses, students, and doctors
who made up the bulk of the house were already un-
sympathetic to the actors because of the long wait for
the curtain to be pulled aside when they could have
spent longer over their dinner. Only the cast, who (with
the exception of Benskin) had been going strongly at
the beer, thought themselves devilishly funny.

The opening chorus successfully defied the audience
to make out a word of it, then Grimsdyke told a joke
about a student and two nurses that extracted a languid
round of clapping. The next item was Benskin's con-
juring act. He appeared in a black cape and a tall
magician's hat, and scored instant applause when,
during his preliminary patter, John Bottle was seized
with the idea of setting a match to its peak over the top
of the backcloth. The hat blazed away for some seconds
before Benskin realized what had happened and angrily
put it out in a bowl of goldfish.

His proudest trick was pouring water from one jug
to another and changing its colour in the transference;
but his aim was not good that afternoon and at his first
attempt most of the liquid slopped on to the ward floor.

'Nurse!' came an easily audible hiss from the back.
It was Sister Fortitude. 'Go and clear up the mess that
young man's making!'

A nurse with a mop picked her way through the
audience and started swabbing round the performer's
feet while he pretended that he, out of everybody else
in the room, did not notice her. After that he angrily
produced a string of flags out of a top hat and left the
stage in a huff.

The rest of the performance was received by the audience with good-natured apathy. Harris made his appearance to sing Little Polly Perkins in a Harry Tate moustache, standing in front of Bottle, Sprogget, and Benskin, who joined in the choruses. Towards the end of the third verse a roar of laughter swept the audience. Harris felt the glow of success in his heart, and sang on lustily. When the laughter rose to a second peak a few seconds later he hesitated and glanced behind him. The cause of his reception was obvious at once. Benskin, finally overcome, had been suffering a sharp attack of hiccoughs before being sick in the corner of the stage. At that moment the lights fused, and no one thought it worth finishing the performance.

*　　*　　*　　*　　*

At Christmas-time came the few hours of every year that the official barrier between students and nurses was gingerly raised: there was a dance in the nurses' dining-hall which the young men were allowed to attend.

The dance disorganized life in the Virgins' Retreat for some weeks before the French chalk went down on the floor. Each nurse's escort was discussed in detail that would have been justified only if the young lady expected to remain in his arms for the rest of her life. Dresses were cleaned, repaired, and borrowed, and the probationers wept in front of their mirrors at the devastation already done to their figures by the carbohydrates in the hospital diet and the muscular exercise of nursing. On the evening of the dance the girls flew off duty eagerly, bathed, powdered, dressed, and scented themselves, and went down to meet their men under the marble eye of Florence Nightingale in the hall.

As I had no particular attachments in the hospital at the time I approached a gawky nurse on the ward called Footte and asked, with a smirk, if she would be my consort. She gave her gracious acceptance. Shortly afterwards I met Benskin in the courtyard.

'Are you going to the nurses' hop?' I asked him. 'I've just let myself in for taking the junior staff on Prudence.'

'You bet I am, old boy! Having recovered from the excesses of Christmas Day I shall be taking old Rigor Mortis along. It's the biggest party of the year.'

I was surprised.

'Is it? I thought it was a strictly teetotal affair.'

'And so it is. You don't imagine the Matron would allow liquor to befoul the chaste floors of the Virgins' Retreat, do you? It's as dry as a bishop's birthday. This has the effect of making everybody get a big enough glow on beforehand to last them the night, and results in some interesting spectacles.'

On the evening of the dance Benskin and I spent an hour of determined drinking with the Padre before crossing over to the Nurses' Home to meet our partners. Benskin immediately suggested a few scoops. 'Bad form to arrive too early, you know,' he explained to the girls. 'People think you want to hog all the sausage rolls.' The four of us went back to the King George, which was now full of young men and young women in evening dress taking prophylaxis against a dull evening. We settled ourselves at a corner of the bar. After some time Miss Footte started looking mistily at me and stroking the back of my neck; I noticed that even Rigor Mortis, who had an apparent amnesia about the incident in the flat, was becoming mildly animated.

The first time I looked at my watch it was after ten.
'It's getting on,' I said. 'Hadn't we better go?'

'Perhaps we'd better. Where's the Padre?' Benskin
leaned over the bar counter. 'Padre! I say, how
about a little this-and-that for the hip?' He handed a
silver flask across the bar. 'There's a long way to go
yet.'

'Certainly, sir! How about you, Mr. Gordon? If I
might advise you, sir, from my experience . . .'

'I'll have a bottle of gin,' I said. 'Can you put it on
the slate until the New Year?'

'Of course, Mr. Gordon. You get your allowance
quarterly, don't you? Anything you like, sir.'

Arm in arm, all four, we went singing to the Nurses'
Home.

The gaunt dining-hall was dripping with paper
chains, and a five-piece band was stuck up on a tinsel-
ringed dais in one corner. There was a Christmas tree,
a running buffet on trestles, streamers, paper hats,
Chinese lanterns, and all the standardized trappings of
respectable jollity. On a stage at one end, opposite the
band, there sat throughout the evening the Matron, in
full uniform. Next to her, also uniformed, were the
three sister tutors. Behind them were five or six of the
senior sisters in a row, and the lot were separated by
sandwiches and sausage rolls on small tables. They
were a jury that was constantly forming unspoken
verdicts. Very little escaped them. If a girl danced with
too many men or too few it was remembered until the
end of her training, and if she turned up in an off-the-
shoulder gown she might as well have had 'Hussy'
tattooed across her clavicles.

There was an interval between dances when we
arrived. We pushed our way up to the buffet.

'Look at that!' Benskin said in disgust, pointing to a row of glass jugs. 'Lemonade!'

He reached across the table and picked up a half-full pitcher.

'I think we might stiffen this a little,' he continued, with a shifty glance over his shoulder towards the stage. 'Hold the jug, old boy, while I get my flask out.'

He tipped his flask of whisky into the drink and I added half my bottle of gin.

'That should be more like it,' Benskin said with satisfaction, stirring the mixture with a jelly spoon. 'Guaranteed to bring the roses to the cheeks. One sip, and never a dull moment afterwards.'

He was still stirring when Mike Kelly appeared at the table with one of the operating theatre nurses.

'Mind if we join the party, Tony?' he asked. 'I've got some rum in my pocket.'

'Put it in, old boy!' Benskin invited him. 'Nothing like a lemonade cocktail to get the party going. That's right, pour the lot in. You didn't have much left, anyway.'

'The best part of half a bottle!' Kelly said indignantly. 'It's all I've got, too.'

'Fear nothing,' Benskin said, stirring rapidly. 'I know of secret caches. Now! Let us taste the devil's brew.'

He poured a little in six glasses and we sipped it with some foreboding.

'It's strong,' Benskin admitted, gulping. 'Odd sort of taste. I suppose that rum was all right, Mike? You hadn't been palmed off with a bottle of hooch, had you?'

'Of course it was all right. I got it off the Padre.'

'Oh well, it must be the lemonade. Cheers, everyone.'

We had almost finished the jug when Harris pushed his way into the group.

'You dirty dogs!' he exclaimed angrily. 'You've pinched my blasted jug of lemonade! I had half a bottle of sherry and some crème de menthe in that, too!'

*   *   *   *   *

I did not remember much about the dance. Isolated incidents came back to me in flashes the next day, like fragments of a dream. I recalled two gentlemen doing the old-fashioned waltz with their partners, catching the tails of their coats together, and covering the floor with broken glass and the best part of two bottles of gin; other gentlemen overcome with the heat and having to be assisted to the fresh air; nurse Footte laughing so loudly in my arms I noticed her uvula waggling in the back of her throat, and my thinking how horrible it was. All the students were drunk, and the Matron, being unaware of such things, beamed and thought she was giving these high-spirited young men a great evening. The next morning, however, she democratically joined in cleaning the hall herself and was horrified to find a hundred and thirty empty spirit bottles tucked away in the potted palms, behind the curtains, in the seats of the sofas, and on top of the framed portraits of her predecessors in office.

The nurses' dance marked the end of the Christmas holiday at St. Swithin's. Everyone knew that the next morning the operating theatres would start work again, new patients would be admitted, lectures would begin, and the students would troop round the bare and gloomy wards with their Chiefs. But that night it was still Christmas, and the hospital was alive with marauding students who leaped on the night nurses while they made cocoa in the ward kitchens. And they, dear girls, screamed softly (so as not to wake the patients) before surrendering themselves to their students' arms. After all, there had to be some compensations for being a nurse.

12

IN the New Year I began work in the out-patient department. It was my first contact with the hard routine of the general practitioner's surgery. In the wards the patients are scrubbed, combed, and undressed, and presented to the doctors in crisp sheets; but in out-patients' they came straight off the streets and examination is complicated by clothes, embarrassment, and sometimes the advisability of the medical attendant keeping his distance.

The department was the busiest part of the hospital. It was centred round a wide, high green-painted hall decorated only by coloured Ministry of Health posters warning the populace against the danger of spitting, refusing to have their babies inoculated, cooking greens in too much water, and indiscriminate love-making. There led off from the hall, on all sides, the assortment of clinics that it had been found necessary to establish to treat the wide variety of illnesses carried in through the doors every day. There were the big medical and surgical rooms, the gynæcological department and the ante-natal clinic, the ear, nose, and throat clinic, the fracture clinic, and a dozen others. The V.D. department was approached through discreet and unmarked entrances from the street; in one corner the infertility clinic and the birth control clinic stood next to one another; and at the other end of the hall were the shady confessionals of the psychiatrists.

On one side was a long counter, behind which four or five girls in white smocks sorted the case notes from their filing cabinets and passed them across to the patients with the carefully cultivated air of distaste mixed with suspicion employed by Customs men handing back passports. There were telephones in the middle of the hall for emergency calls, and, outside every clinic door, rows of wooden benches that looked as inviting to sit on as a line of tank-traps.

The department was run chiefly by the hospital porters. These were an invaluable body of men, without whom the work of the hospital would immediately have come to a standstill. They were experts at such common tasks beyond the ability of the doctors as directing patients to the correct department, holding down drunks, putting on strait-jackets, dealing tactfully with the police, getting rid of unwanted relatives, and finding cups of tea at impossible hours. They stood, in their red and blue livery, inspecting with experienced Cockney shrewdness the humanity that daily passed in large numbers under their noses.

As soon as a patient entered the building he came up against a porter—a fat one sitting on a stool behind a high desk, like a sergeant in the charge-room of a police station.

'What's up, chum?' the porter demanded.

The patient would begin to mumble out his leading symptoms, but he would be cut short with 'Surgical, you,' or 'Throat department,' or the name of the appropriate clinic. The porters were the best diagnosticians in the hospital. They unerringly divided the cases into medical and surgical so that the patients arrived in front of the correct specialist. If a porter had made a mistake and consigned, for instance, a case of bronchitis to the surgical side, the complications that would have arisen and the disaster that might have overtaken the patient were beyond speculation.

After passing the porter the patient visited the counter to collect his case notes. St. Swithin's kept faithful records of its visitors, and several residents of the district had been neatly represented by a green folder containing the obstetrical notes of his birth, an account of the removal of his tonsils, the surgical description of the repair of his hernias, a record of his mounting blood pressure, and details of the post-mortem following the final complaint that carried him off. Clutching his folder in one hand, he took his place at the end of the queue seated outside the door of his clinic. The queue shifted up the wooden seat as each patient was called inside by the stern-faced nurse at the door: the movement was slow and spasmodic, like the stirrings of a sleepy snake.

For the first half-hour the patient amused himself by reading carefully through his folder of confidential notes, comparing in his mind what the doctors had written about him with what they told him to his face. After a while this became boring, so he read the morning paper. When he had exhausted the paper, he passed the remainder of the time in clinical discussion with his neighbours. This was the most attractive part of the visit, and a pleasure he had been storing up for himself.

Discussion of one's illness with neighbours on the bench was done with pride: the patients wore their symptoms like a row of campaign medals.

'Wot you in for, cock?' he began to the man next to him.

' 'Art trouble,' was the reply, delivered with gloomy zest.

'Anyfink else?'

'That's enough, ain't it?' replied the neighbour sharply. ' 'Ow about you?'

'The doctor says I am a walking pathological museum.' The patient rolled the syllables off his tongue deliberately.

'Go on!'

'I've got diabetes mellitus, 'emeroids, normocytic anæmia, chronic bronchitis and emphysema, 'ammer toe, cholecystitis, and an over-active thyroid.'

'That's a packet, all right,' his neighbour admitted grudgingly.

'And I 'eard 'im say I've got a positive Wasserman, too!' he added in triumph.

' 'Ave you 'ad any operations?' inquired a thin woman on the other side of him in a voice rich with misery.

'Not to date, touch wood, I 'aven't.'

The woman gave a loud sigh.

'I wish as I could say the same,' she remarked, shaking her head sadly.

' 'Ow many 'ave you 'ad, missus?' asked the patient, anxious over his own record.

'Fifteen,' she told him, in tones of exquisite martyrdom.

'Coo! I'm glad I 'aven't got your complaint.'

'That's the trouble. They don't know wot's wrong with me. The last time they took out my colon. The doctor said it was the worst they'd ever 'ad in the 'ospital. Took them four and a 'arf hours, it did. Then they 'ad to leave some of it behind. I'm lucky to be 'ere now, if you ask me.'

'Must have been a bad do,' the patient said, respectful of such exuberant pathology.

'Bad do! I was left to die four times!'

' 'Oo's your doctor, missus?'

'Mr. Cambridge. Wot a lovely man! 'E's got such soft 'ands.'

I soon discovered another peculiarity of out-patient work. In the wards the patients are all ill: in out-patients' they are nearly all healthy. Men and women with organic disease formed a small fraction of the hundreds who came past the fat porter at the door every day. Most of them complained of vague aches and pains that they had been trotting up to the surgeries of their own doctors for several months, and they, poor men, had got rid of them temporarily by handing them a note to St. Swithin's. This was an example of an established medical practice known as snag-shifting, which went on just as actively in St. Swithin's itself.

The most usual condition in out-patients' was headache, which was slightly more common than troubles of the poor feet, giddy spells, the rheumatics, and insomnia ('Not a wink for forty years, doctor'). Most of the symptoms were manifestly incompatible with life if they had existed, but every patient had to be investigated in case something sinister lay beneath. This provided an excellent opportunity for snag-shifting. A persistent patient with headaches could, with a few strokes of the pen, be transferred to the eye department. It simply needed the houseman to scribble 'Headaches. Any eye signs?' on the notes and the patient moved to another queue outside another doctor's door. After the eye department had found nothing and were tired of the fellow appearing in front of them week after week they sent him to the throat clinic. The throat surgeons usually operated on all their patients and would probably remove his tonsils or the inside of his sinuses; when he continued to attend with his headaches afterwards, they would pack him off to the general surgeons with the suggestion his complaint was the result of sepsis lurking in his gall-bladder, kidney, or some other organ comfortably outside their province. The surgeons might operate or not, according to the length of their waiting-list at the time; whatever happened, after a few more visits to out-patients' he would find himself having all his teeth out in the dental section, who packed him off afterwards to the physiotherapy department in case the headaches—which continued—were due to disfunction of the neck muscles. From the physiotherapy department the patient went as a last resort to the psychiatrists, and as they were then unable to transfer him to anyone he probably continued to visit them and talk about his headaches once a week for the remainder of his life.

While I was working in out-patients' the hospital authorities installed a bar for tea and buns in the hall to break the tedium of the long wait. The regular patients were delighted, and showed their appreciation by spending as many of their afternoons as they could enjoying a medical tea-party with their fellow sufferers.

'Times have changed,' one of the old porters said gloomily, looking at the girl distributing cups of tea from the new counter. 'None of this 'ere nonsense in the old days. Mollycoddling, I call it.'

He wistfully described the routine of forty years ago. The patients had to be inside the building and seated at the benches by eight o'clock every morning. Then the doors were locked and anyone coming late had no alternative than to wait until the next day. The consultant arrived at nine, and strode to his room accompanied by a senior porter. When the doctor had settled himself in his chair the porter went to the door and shouted: 'Nah then! All them with coughs, stand up!' A handful of patients came to their feet and shuffled into the room. When they had been seen the porter returned and commanded: 'Stomach pains, diarrhœa, and flatulence!' The possessors of these alimentary disorders filed before the doctor while the porter marshalled the chronic cases who had come simply for a new bottle of medicine. The patients found the system convenient, and it was abolished only when the senior physician left for Harley Street after a re-markably heavy morning treating chest symptoms and found a stall outside the hospital from which was being sold 'Genuine St. Swithin's Cough Mixture.' This was bought off the patients for twopence and retailed to the public by the stallkeeper at sixpence a bottle.

We each spent two days a week in the accident room, where I began to feel I was at last learning a little medicine by discovering how to put a bandage on without dropping it on the floor, to sew up cuts, to remove foreign bodies from eyes, and to apply a kaolin poultice. A pair of us were obliged to sleep once a week in a couple of bunks in a small room by the accident entrance, to attend the minor injuries that trickled in unendingly during the night. This system was nearly the end of Tony Benskin. In his wanderings round the sleeping hospital he had met, and taken a fancy to, one of the night nurses, and turned himself into a red-eyed wreck all day by sitting most of the night in her company.

The conditions in a ward at night are admittedly

lightly aphrodisiac. The nurse sits alone at one end of the long room, which melts away on each side into shadows and is illuminated only by a single red-shaded lamp on the desk in front of her. The soft warm light makes her as desirable as a ripe peach. There is not much room at the desk, so the student and nurse sit close together. To avoid disturbing the patients they must whisper, which turns every remark into an intimacy. They are the only two awake in a sleeping world and they draw together with a tingling sense of isolation.

The nurse mixes the student a milk drink from the patients' night rations. It is surprising what can occur in such conditions over a couple of cups of Horlicks. Their knees touch under the desk; their hands brush together in a determined accident; their fingers entwine and they sweat into one another's palms until the night sister is due on her round. The student pours soft endearments over the girl like treacle on a pudding, though his technique is sometimes ruined by his being interrupted in a delicate submission to her charms by a rough voice from the nearest bed demanding 'Can I 'ave the bedpan please, nurse?'

Benskin's romance might have ended harmlessly if it had not been for a lapse on the last night of our appointment. We were on duty together, and to celebrate the end of the session we persuaded the casualty nurse to do our work and spent the evening in the King George. At closing time Benskin rushed to see his night nurse, while I flopped into bed.

Just after three I was shaken awake. Automatically I reached for my trousers, thinking it was the porter demanding my attendance in the accident room: but it was Benskin. He was in a pitiful state.

'Old man!' he said urgently. 'You've got to help me! Something terrible's happened!'

I tried to concentrate on the disaster.

'What's up?' I asked sleepily.

'You know that girl up in the ward—Molly. Remember, the one I've been popping up to see?'

'Umm.'

'Well—listen, old man, don't go to sleep for God's sake! To-night I nipped up to see her as usual, and I was brimming over a bit with the old joys of spring and so forth owing to being full of beer. . . .'

'Disgusting.'

'. . . and Christ Almighty, before I knew where I was I'd proposed to the bloody woman!'

I tried to clear sleep and alcohol out of my eyes, like soapsuds.

'Did she accept?' I asked, yawning.

'Accept! She said "Yes, please," as far as I remember. Don't you realize what's happened? Can't you see the gravity of the situation?'

'Perhaps she'll have forgotten by the morning,' I suggested hopefully.

'Not on your life! You know what these women are— at night nurses' breakfast it'll be a case of "Guess what, girls! Tony Benskin proposed to me at last and we're going to be married in May!" Oh God, oh God!' He clasped his head. 'It'll be all round the hospital by nine o'clock.'

'I gather you're not keen on the idea of marrying her?'

'Me! Married! Can you see it?' he exclaimed.

I nodded my head understandingly and propped myself up on an elbow.

'This needs some thought.'

'How right you are!'

'Surely there must be something you can do . . can't you go back and explain it was all in fun?'

Benskin gave a contemptuous laugh.

'You go,' he said.

'I see your point. It's tricky. Let's think in silence.'

After about twenty minutes I had an idea. I criticized it to myself carefully and it seemed sound.

'I think I've got the answer,' I said, and explained it to him.

He leapt to his feet, shook me warmly by the hand, and hurried back to the ward.

The solution was a simple one. I sent Benskin round to propose to every night nurse in the hospital.

13

THE clock on the lecture-room wall crept towards ten past four: the Professor of Pathology had overrun his time again.

It was a gloomy, overcast afternoon at the beginning of April. The lights were reflected from the brown varnish on the walls in dull yellow pools. The windows just below the ceiling were, as usual, shut tight, and the air was narcotic. The students packing the tiers of uncomfortable benches were sleepy, annoyed at being kept late, and waiting for their tea.

The Professor was unconscious of the passage of time, the atmosphere in the room, or the necessity for food and drink. He was a thin little white-haired man with large spectacles who was standing behind his desk talking enthusiastically about a little-known variety of louse. Lice were the Professor's life. For thirty years they had filled his thoughts during the day and spilled into his dreams at night. He had, at points during that time, married and raised five children, but he was only faintly aware of these occurrences. The foreground of his mind was filled by lice. He spent his time in his own small laboratory on the top floor of the hospital wholly occupied in studying their habits. He rarely came near his students. He left the teaching to his assistants and considered he had done his share by occasionally wandering round the students' laboratory, which he did with the bemused air of a man whose wife has invited a lot of people he doesn't know to a party. He insisted, however, on giving to each class a series of lectures on his speciality. He was the greatest authority on lice in the world, and when he lectured to other pathologists in Melbourne, Chicago, Oslo, or Bombay, men would eagerly cross half a continent to hear him. But the students of his own hospital, who had only the effort of shifting themselves out of the sofas in the common room, came ungracefully and ungratefully, and found it all rather boring.

As the lecturer droned on, describing the dispro-portionately complicated sexual habits of an obscure species of louse, the students glanced sullenly at the clock, shuffled their feet, yawned, folded up their note-books, put away their pens, and lolled in their seats. Some of the class started chatting to their neighbours or lit their pipes and read the evening paper as com-fortably as if they were sitting in their own lodgings. From the back row came a subdued stamping of feet on the wooden floor—the students' only means of retaliation on their lecturers. But the Professor had by now forgotten the presence of his audience and if we had all marched out into the fresh air or set the lecture theatre on fire he would have noticed it only dimly.

I was sitting at the back with Tony Benskin and Sprogget. Benskin always took a place as far back as he could, for some lecturers had the unpleasant habit of asking questions of students who were dreamily inspect-ing the ceiling and at a distance it was possible to give the impression of overpowering concentration even if asleep. It was also convenient for making an exit un-obtrusively when the lecturer became insupportably boring. Attendance at lectures was compulsory at St. Swithin's, and a board was passed round the benches for each student to record his presence by signing it. This led to everyone in the medical school rapidly becoming competent in forgery, so that the absence of a friend could easily be rectified. This unselfish practice diminished after the Dean counted the students at his own lecture and found not only that thirty-odd men were represented by ninety signatures but that some of the absentees had in their enthusiasm forgetfully signed the board in different places four times.

The Professor had left me behind some time ago. I was cleaning my nails, letting my thoughts wander pleasantly to the comfortable drone of the lecturer's voice. Unfortunately, in their wanderings they stumbled across a topic I wished they could have avoided.

'I say, Tony,' I asked softly. 'I suppose you couldn't lend me three or four quid, could you?'

Benskin laughed—so loudly that men in the three rows in front of him turned round.

'I thought not,' I said. 'All the same, it's damned difficult. Now we've started the path. course I've got to have my microscope back. While we were in the wards it was perfectly all right for it to lodge in Goldstein's window, but if I don't get it soon I shan't be able to do the practical classes at all.'

'I sympathize,' Benskin said. 'Have no doubts about that. My own instrument is at present locked in the coffers of Mr. Goldstein's rival down the road, and I see no prospect of recovering it from the clutches of said gentleman at all. The old money-bags are empty. For weeks now I've had to wait outside the bank until the manager goes to lunch before cashing a cheque.'

My microscope was an easy way of raising ready

money; I could pawn it without inconvenience when broke and reclaim it the moment my allowance came in. But I had recently piled up so many other commitments that this simple system had broken down. My tastes had altered expensively since I first arrived at St. Swithin's, though my allowance had stayed much the same. Then I smoked a little, drank hardly at all, and never went out with girls; now I did all three together.

'The funny thing is, old man,' said Benskin when the Professor had exhausted the educational qualities of lice, 'that I was just thinking of putting the leeches on you for a quid or so. The cost of living is extremely high with me at the moment. I suppose there really is no possibility of a small loan?'

'None at all.'

'I must raise a little crinkly from somewhere. Surely one of the students has a couple of bob he can jingle in his pocket?'

'You can try Grimsdyke,' I suggested. 'He usually has a bit left over for his friends.'

Benskin frowned. 'Not since he got married, old boy. The little woman takes a dim view of the stuff being diverted from the housekeeping to the pockets of old soaks. No, there's nothing for it—it's a case of bashing the old dishes again.'

All of us had recurrent bouts of insolvency, and each had his favourite way of raising enough money to pay his debts. Dishwashing by the night was the most popular way of earning small sums, as it did not interfere with classes, it could be taken up without notice, and the big hotels and restaurants in London paid comparatively well for a few hours spent in the stillroom. Baby-sitting was Sprogget's speciality, and John Bottle occasionally brought home a few pounds from the tote or by winning the waltz competition at an Oxford Street palais. But Benskin sometimes overspent himself so much that more settled employment had to be found. One afternoon during a time when he was suffering a severe attack of poverty he appeared in the students' common room in his best blue serge suit, with his shoes brightly polished, his hair neat, a white handkerchief smartly in his pocket, and a plain peaked cap in his hand.

'What on earth are you doing?' Grimsdyke asked. 'Playing bus conductors?'

Benskin beamed at him.

'Not a bit, old boy. I've got a job for a couple of weeks. A damn smart move on my part it was.'

'A job? What sort of a job? More dishwashing, I suppose?'

'Private chauffeur,' Benskin told him proudly. 'In a Rolls, too. I'll tell you what happened. I was up at out-patients' this morning when a fellow came in with the most horrible gastric ulcer I've seen. He had to leave off work at once, of course, and when he told me his job was chauffeur to an old bird with bags of oof who makes jam or something I saw ways of relieving the old exchequer. Do you follow me? I nipped smartly round to the old boy's house in Hampstead and told him the bad news in person—very impressively, too. I then explained the situation in a few words, and offered humble self to fill the gap in his household.

'It so happened that the old chum and his missus are due to start a fortnight's holiday touring Scotland to-morrow, which would have been squashed by the chauffeur's ulcers if I hadn't presented myself as a worthy alternative. I got all this from the patient of course, but I didn't let on and gave the impression that

I could tear myself away from my valuable studies just so the old folk wouldn't miss their nice restful holiday. He seemed a decent old cove and was very upset about his old chauffeur, but he has no more idea of driving a car himself than working a railway engine. So my offer was gratefully accepted.'

'Have you got a licence?' I asked him.

'Of course,' he replied in a hurt tone. 'For almost a month now.'

Benskin disappeared the following morning. After four days he reappeared in the hospital. He had lost his cap, his best suit was torn and covered with oil, one of his shoes was ripped, and he was still broke.

'Well?' I said.

'One meets snags,' Benskin replied in a subdued voice. 'All was well to begin with. The old jam merchant was a great believer in the quiet life, and we trundled gently out of Town to Doncaster. They put me up in the servants' quarters of the local hostelry, where I met a hell of a nice little piece among the chambermaids— however, that will do for later. The next day I drove in an exemplary fashion to Newcastle, by which time I could see that the old couple had invested plenty of confidence in Benskin, whom they looked upon as a clean and careful driver.'

'What happened after Newcastle?' Grimsdyke asked resignedly.

'That's where the rot set in. I'd driven all that bloody way without a drink, as I left London flat broke. At Newcastle I touched the old boy for a quid, and when we stopped for lunch at some old-world boozer on the road I sneaked round the back and downed a few scoops. This would have been all right, but the old chum decided he wanted a stroll to look at the local countryside and left me among the lackeys in the servants' hall or whatever it is. I met a most amusing type there—an Irish porter who had started off life studying divinity at Trinity. We had a lot to talk about —bobbing back scoops all the time, of course. I set off with my customers about four o'clock, but regret to say I only made about a hundred yards. After that I piled the crate up in a ditch. I didn't hurt myself, luckily, but now the old couple are languishing in the local cottage hospital with a fractured femur apiece.'

He added that he did not see much chance of the engagement being renewed.

*   *   *   *   *

To retrieve my microscope I washed dishes with Tony Benskin in a West End hotel for a couple of nights and sold some of my text-books. I was then content to return to academic life, but Benskin was aflame to increase his savings by trying his hand at another trade.

'Do you see that notice?' he asked eagerly as we left the staff entrance of the hotel in the early morning. ' "Extra waiters wanted. Apply Head Waiter." That's an idea, isn't it?'

'No,' I said. 'I'm going to spend a few nights in bed. Besides, I don't know anything about waiting. And neither do you.'

Benskin lightly brushed these objections aside.

'There's nothing to it, old man. Anyone can dish up a bit of fish. It's money for nothing, if you ask me. And the tips! Think of the tips. At a swep-up joint like this the customers don't slip threepenny bits under the plate when they swig down the remains of their brandy and wipe the caviar off their lips. I've been waited on quite long enough to grasp the technique—if you want a fat tip it's only a matter of handing out the soup with a look of haughty distaste on your face.'

'You think you could look haughty, do you?'

'One is a gentleman,' Benskin replied stiffly. 'I'm going to stay behind and have a word with this head waiter chap.'

'I'm going home to bed. We've got to appear at a lecture in five hours' time.'

'All right. See you later.'

I was dropping off to sleep when Benskin got back to Bayswater. He was jubilant.

'A push-over, old boy!' he said. 'I saw the head waiter—a nasty piece of work he was, too. However, he took one look at me and said to himself "Benskin's the man! He'll raise the tone in the dining-room all right." '

'So you got the job?'

'Starting to-night. I'll just have time to nip away from the hospital, get my evening clothes out, and appear as the Jeeves of the chafing dish.'

'I suppose they know at the hotel that you have had no experience of waiting at all?'

'Well, no, not exactly. I saw no reason for putting obstacles in my own way, so I gave the impression I had dished it out at some of the larger doss-houses around Town, with summer sessions on the coast. They seem pretty hard-up for fish-flingers at the moment, as they took me at my word.'

'Well,' I said, turning over. 'Don't forget to wear a black tie.'

When I reached the flat after work that evening Benskin was in a high state of excitement.

'Must get the old soup and fish out,' he said, hauling his battered tin trunk from the top of the wardrobe.

'I pinched a bottle of ether from the theatre this afternoon to get the stains out.'

Benskin's tail suit had been bought for him by his father when he was sixteen. Since then he had greatly increased in size in all directions. We all worked hard to straighten out the creases with John Bottle's travelling iron, while Benskin rubbed hard at the lapels to remove the grease.

'I must have been a dirty little devil at table,' he reflected.

'Some moths have been having a go at it down here,' I said, pointing to the trousers.

'That doesn't matter,' Benskin replied testily. 'I'm only the bloody waiter, anyway.'

He put the clothes on. By lowering the braces as far as he dared the trousers could be made to cover the upper part of his ankles; the braces themselves, which were red and yellow, only remained invisible behind the lapels of the coat when he remembered not to breathe too deeply. The sleeves came as far as the mid-forearm, and the top buttons of the trousers had to be reinforced with safety-pins. But it was the shirt that presented an apparently insoluble difficulty. It was tight, and the buttonholes were worn: even the shallowest of respirations caused the studs to pop out and expose a broad strip of hairy, pink, sweaty chest.

'Quite enough to put the people off their meal,' John Bottle remarked.

We tried using bigger studs and brass paper-fasteners, but, if Benskin wished to continue to breathe, the shirt was unwearable. Even strips of sticking-plaster inside the stiff front were not strong enough to withstand the pressure of his inhalations. For half an hour we worked hard at the infuriating gap while the shirt-front became limp under our fingers.

'For God's sake!' Benskin exclaimed angrily. 'Isn't there anything we can do about it? Look at the time! If I'm not there in twenty minutes I've had it. Surely one of you fellows has got a stiff shirt to lend me?'

'What! Your size?' Bottle asked.

'Why the devil didn't I think of buying a dickey!'

I had an idea.

'Let us apply the first principles of surgery,' I said.

'What the hell are you getting at now?'

'Supposing you have tension on a surgical incision. What do you do? Why, make a counter-incision, of course, in a site where it doesn't matter. Take your jacket off, Tony.'

A quick rip with the scissors up the length of the shirt-back from the tail to the collar and Benskin was once again the perfect English gentleman. He left the flat in high spirits, convinced that he would make enough in the evening to keep him in drinks for a fortnight. Unhappily he was no better at serving hot soup than driving a car and was dismissed by the furious maître d'hôtel between the fish and the entrée.

14

'B.I.D.,' I said. 'Brought in dead. What an epitaph!'

I was standing in the cold, bright post-mortem room on the top floor of the hospital. It was a large room with a glass roof, tiles round the walls, three heavy porcelain tables, and one side made up of a bank of numbered metal drawers like the front of a large filing cabinet. The unfortunate patients were brought by the cheery-looking fellow on his trolley to a special lift, taken to the roof, and packed away neatly in the refrigerated drawers. Each corpse bore a label giving the name, religion, and diagnosis, but the man on the table in front of me had only the three letters on his tab. He had been picked up in the street by the police a few hours before and brought futilely to the accident room.

I pulled the heavy rubber gloves tight and began my incision with the big post-mortem knife. I never liked doing post-mortems. They made me feel sick. However, under the medical school regulations I was required to perform three of them, so I had to get on with it.

Every morning at twelve the physicians and surgeons came up to the room to see their unsuccessful cases demonstrated by the heartless pathologist. Often they had been right in life, and had the satisfaction of feeling with their fingers the lesion they had built up in their imagination from examination of the body surface, deduction, and studying the black and grey shadows on X-ray films. Occasionally they were humbled.

'So there *was* a tumour of the cerebellum after all!' I once heard Dr. Malcolm Maxworth exclaim, going red in the face. 'Damn it, damn it, damn it!'

Maxworth was not angry on the dead patient's behalf: it was simply that in the daily contest between his mind and the tricks of the body the body had for once won a game.

Our afternoons were spent wandering round the dusty pathology museum inspecting the grotesque specimens in the big glass jars of spirit. They had everything in the St. Swithin's museum, from two-headed babies to tattoo marks. Each specimen was neatly labelled and numbered, and a clinical history of the case was set out on a card attached to the bottle. 'How much better than a tombstone!' Grimsdyke said as he read the last dramatic illness of John O'Hara in 1927 and held the remains of his ruptured aneurism in his hand. 'I suppose everyone wants to be remembered somehow. What could be better than giving a bit of yourself to the pathologists? Nobody knows or cares where this fellow's grave is, but his memory is kept fresh in here almost daily. A whopping aneurism! I bet it caused a panic in the ward when it burst.'

Twice a week during the three-month pathology course we had classes in forensic medicine. This was a subject that fascinated me, because I was a conscientious reader of detective stories and took delight in the realization that I too now knew how to distinguish human blood from animal's, compare bullet wounds, and differentiate murder from suicide. The lecturer was a portly, genial man whose picture appeared fairly regularly in the

Sunday papers inspecting the scene of all the more attractive crimes. We learnt from him the favourite ways of committing suicide, abortion, homicide, and rape: the lecture on the last subject, which was illustrated with lantern slides, was the only one I can remember when I couldn't find a seat.

After the pathology course we began a round of the special departments, spending a few weeks in each. I was sent to learn a little about eyes and then to the throat surgeons, where I learned how to look into ears, up noses, and down throats. The E.N.T. clinic was busy from early morning until long after the others had finished at night, for the London atmosphere silted up patients' sinuses and roughened their lungs. 'That stuff's really irrespirable,' said the surgeon, flinging his arm in the direction of the window. 'Thank God I live in the country.' He was a big, brusque, overworked man who had nevertheless extracted a fortune from the respiratory damage caused by London air. He was supposed to be the fastest remover of tonsils and adenoids in the country, which he did every Thursday afternoon in out-patients', passing the anæsthetized children through his hands with the efficiency of a Chicago pig-killer.

After the throat department I was glad to sink into the restful atmosphere of the skin clinic. This was run by two very old and very gentlemanly specialists who conversed with each other, the students, the nurses, and the patients in whispers. They were both formally dressed in expensive suits, and each arrived at the hospital with a Rolls and a chauffeur. I had not expected such opulence and satisfied tranquillity from dermatologists, but on reflection it struck me that diseases of the skin were the most agreeable of all to specialize in. They are quiet, undramatic affairs which never get you up in the middle of the night nor interrupt your meals. The patients never die, but on the other hand they never seem to get better. A private patient, once diagnosed, is therefore a regular source of income to his doctor for the rest of his long life.

*　　*　　*　　*　　*

I still lived in the flat in Bayswater with Benskin and Bottle. Archie Broom and Mike Kelly had qualified and left, and we had been joined by Sprogget and Evans.

One evening after supper Bottle leant back in his chair and said, 'What shall we do to-night? Could you take a flick, anyone?'

'There's nothing on much,' said Tony in a bored voice. 'We might pop out for a pint a bit later.'

'I've got a novel to finish,' Evans said. 'It's got to go back to the library by the sixteenth. What's the date to-day, John?'

Bottle picked up the calendar from the mantelpiece. 'The fourteenth,' he said. He frowned. 'I say, do you chaps realize it is exactly five weeks to-day to our finals?'

'What!' Benskin jumped up in his chair. 'It can't be. They're not till the end of October.'

'Well, this is the middle of September.'

'Good God!' said Sprogget nervously. 'We shall have to start doing some work.'

Bottle put the calendar back.

'I'm afraid you're right. I've hardly looked at a book since we came out of the anatomy rooms. We've had a bloody good holiday, and now we've got to pay for it.'

Benskin, who believed in making his unpleasant

decisions swiftly, immediately picked up a copy of Price's *Practice of Medicine* from the bookshelf and wiped the dust off the cover with his sleeve.

'At least that settles our evening for us,' he said. 'From now on it's a case of burning the old midnight oil. Good Heavens! Is there all this on tuberculosis?'

Our evenings afterwards were swiftly blown away in a gale of industry. We collected up our dusty books from the floor, the chairs, and the back of the cupboards, and left them in heaps, open, on the table. As soon as we returned from our work in the hospital we started reading. We ate bread and cheese when we felt like it and took caffeine and benzedrine tablets to keep awake. We worked past midnight, sometimes until four in the morning, cramming three years' study into thirty-five nights.

Each of us developed a favourite attitude for concentration. I found I could learn best sitting on a hard chair with my elbows on the table; Benskin was apparently able to absorb knowledge comfortably only if he removed his collar, tie, shoes, belt, and socks and stuck his large pink feet on the mantelpiece. Bottle preferred to take his text-book and sit alone in the lavatory, and Sprogget would pace nervously up and down the narrow hallway repeating under his breath the signs and symptoms of innumerable diseases and giggling grotesquely when he couldn't remember them. Only Evans passed the pre-examination stage in tranquillity. His mind was so efficient he found it necessary to do no more than loll in an armchair and read gently through his text-books as though they were the Sunday papers.

For an hour or so we would work without speaking, filling the room with tobacco smoke. But it was a thin, taut silence, like the skin of an inflated balloon. Benskin was usually the first to break it.

'What the hell's the dose of digitalis?' he asked angrily one night.

'Six grains eight-hourly for three doses, followed by three grains three times a day for two days, and half that dose four times daily for two days,' I replied brightly.

'I'm sure that's not right,' he said. 'It's somewhere round two grains a day.'

'Of course it's right!' I barked at him. 'I've only just learnt it.'

'Richard's right,' said Evans quietly from his chair.

'All right, all right! Don't fly off about it. I haven't got as far as digitalis yet, anyway.'

Sprogget's head appeared at the door.

'Is a presystolic murmur at the apex diagnostic of mitral stenosis?' he asked anxiously.

'Yes,' Evans said.

'Oh damn! I didn't think it was.' He looked as if he was going to burst into tears. 'I'm bound to fail, I know I am!' he exclaimed.

'You'll be all right,' Benskin told him gruffly. 'It's nervous types like me who'll come down. Do you get cyanosis in pneumonia?'

We took one night a week off: on Saturday we all went out and got drunk. The rest of the time we were irritable with each other, uncommunicative, and jumpy. Benskin's usual sunny good humour seemed to have left him for ever. He scowled at his companions, complained about everything in the flat, and developed the symptoms of a gastric ulcer.

The grim period of study and Benskin's bad temper were relieved by only one incident before the examination. One Sunday night the famous helmet disappeared from the King George. No one knew who had taken it and no one had seen it go: it had simply vanished from its hook some time during the evening. The theft made Benskin furious, particularly as he had reasons to suspect the students from Bart's, whom St. Swithin's had beaten soundly earlier on in the year in the inter-hospitals' rugby cup. The next night he took himself off to Smithfield and climbed over the venerable walls of that ancient institution. He didn't find the helmet, but he put his foot through a window and was asked to leave by a porter. His foray came to the ears of the Dean of St. Swithin's, who called him to his office, abused him soundly for ten minutes, and fined him three guineas. The Dean could not appreciate at all Benskin's plea that the loss of the helmet justified such strong action. Whether this had any connection with an event that occurred shortly afterwards and established itself for ever in the hospital tradition with the title of the Dean's Tea Party was never known. Benskin was suspected, and there was a rumour that he had been spotted coming out of a small printer's in the City: but there was never any proof.

A few days after his interview with Benskin the Dean entered his office to find his personal secretary rummaging through his desk.

'Hello!' he said. 'Lost something?'

'Not exactly, sir,' she said, giving him a worried look. 'I was just wondering why I hadn't seen the invitations?'

'Invitations? What invitations?'

'To your At Home to-morrow,' she replied simply. 'The 'phone's been ringing all morning. The Deans of all the other hospitals in London have been through to say that the notice is a little short but they will be glad to come for cocktails in the library. There have been some people from the Medical Research Council, too, and a professor from Birmingham.' She looked at a pencilled list in her hand. 'About thirty have accepted so far, and there looks like a good many more have arrived by the second post.'

The Dean hurled his hat on the floor.

'It's an outrage!' he shouted in fury. 'It's a disgrace! It's a . . . ! By God, these bloody students! By God, I'll punish them for this! You just wait and see!' He poked a quivering finger at her so forcefully she leapt back with a little squeal.

'You mean—it's a hoax?' she asked timidly.

'Of course it's a hoax! It's these damn hooligans we've been giving the best years of our lives trying to educate! Send me the School Secretary! And the Professor of Medicine! Get me the Head Porter! Ring up all those people and tell them the thing's a damnable practical joke!'

'What, all of them?'

'Of course, woman! You don't think I'm going to be made a fool of by my own students, do you? Get on to them at once!'

At that moment the 'phone rang again. She picked it up.

'Hello . . .' she said. 'Yes, he's here now. Certainly. One moment please.'

She turned to the Dean. 'The Lord Mayor's Secretary,' she exclaimed. 'He says the Lord Mayor would be delighted.'

The Dean fell into his armchair like a knocked-out boxer.

'Very well,' he groaned. 'Very well, I know when

I'm beaten. Get me those catering people, whats-is-names, instead.'

The party was a great success. Although the Dean entered the library black with anger he found himself in the middle of so many of his distinguished contemporaries that he mellowed rapidly. Didn't the leading heart specialist in the country grip him by the arm and tell him how much he appreciated his latest paper? Didn't the Lord Mayor himself hint of a donation towards the new library, and, more important, ask for an appointment in Harley Street? Besides, he had quickly seen to it that the expenses would be borne by the Governors. He said a genial good-bye to his last guests as they climbed into their cars in the courtyard. Suddenly he saw Benskin, with his hands in his pockets, grinning at him from the shadow of Lord Larrymore's statue. The Dean's face twisted malignantly.

'Do you know anything about this, damn you?' he demanded.

'Me, sir?' Benskin asked innocently. 'Not at all, sir. I think it may have been someone from Bart's.'

15

To a medical student the final examinations are something like death: an unpleasant inevitability to be faced sooner or later, one's state after which is determined by the care spent in preparing for the event.

The examinations of the United Hospitals Committee are held twice a year in a large dingy building near Harley Street. It shares a hidden Marylebone square with two pubs, a sooty caged garden, an antique shop, and the offices of a society for retrieving fallen women. During most of the year the square is a quiet and unsought thoroughfare, its traffic made up by patrons of the pubs, reclaimed women, and an unhappy-looking man in sandals who since 1931 has passed through at nine each morning carrying a red banner saying 'REPENT FOR YE DIE TO-MORROW.' Every six months this orderly quiet is broken up like a road under a pneumatic drill. Three or four hundred students arrive from every hospital in London and from every medical school in the United Kingdom. Any country that accepts a British qualification is represented. There are brown, bespectacled Indians, invariably swotting until the last minute from Sir Leatherby Tidy's fat and invaluable *Synopsis of Medicine*; jet-black gentlemen from West Africa standing in nervous groups and testing their new fountain-pens; fat, coffee-coloured Egyptians discussing earnestly in their own language fine points of erudite medicine; hearty Australians, New Zealanders, and South Africans showing no more anxiety than if they were waiting for a pub to open; the whole diluted thoroughly by a mob of pale, fairly indifferent, untidy-looking British students conversing in accents from the Welsh valleys to Stirlingshire.

An examination is nothing more than an investigation of a man's knowledge, conducted in a way that the authorities have found to be the most fair and convenient to both sides. But the medical student cannot see it in this light. Examinations touch off his fighting spirit; they are a straight contest between himself and the examiners, conducted on well-established rules for both, and he goes at them like a prize-fighter.

There is rarely any frank cheating in medical examinations, but the candidates spend almost as much time over the technical details of the contest as they do learning general medicine from their text-books. We found the papers set for the past ten years in the hospital library, and the five of us carefully went through the questions.

'It's no good wasting time on pneumonia, infant diarrhoea, or appendicitis,' Benskin said. 'They were asked last time. I shouldn't think it's worth learning about T.B. either, it's come up twice in the past three years.'

We all agreed that it was unnecessary to equip ourselves with any knowledge of the most frequent serious illnesses we would come across in practice.

'I tell you what we *ought* to look up,' said Evans. 'Torulosis.'

'Never heard of it,' Benskin said.

'It's pretty rare. But I see that old Macready-Jones is examining this time, and it's his speciality. He has written a lot of stuff about it in the *B.M.J.* and the *Lancet*. He might quite easily pop a question in.'

'All right,' I said. 'I'll look it up in the library to-morrow.'

My chances of meeting a case of torulosis after qualification were remote, and I wouldn't have recognized it if I had. But to be well informed about torulosis in the next fortnight might make the difference between passing and failure.

Benskin discovered that Malcolm Maxworth was the St. Swithin's representative on the Examining Committee and thenceforward we attended all his ward rounds, standing at the front and gazing at him like impressionable music enthusiasts at the solo violinist. The slightest hint he was believed to have dropped was passed round, magnified, and acted upon. Meanwhile, we despondently ticked the days off the calendar, swotted up the spot questions, and ran a final breathless sprint down the well-trodden paths of medicine, snatching handfuls of knowledge from the sides where we could.

*   *   *   *   *

The examination is split into three sections, each one of which must be passed on its own. First there are the written papers, then *viva voce* examinations, and finally the clinical, when the student is presented with a patient and required to turn in a competent diagnosis in half an hour.

On the morning the examination began the five of us left the Bayswater flat early, took a bus along Oxford

Street, and walked towards the examination building in a silent, sickly row. I always found the papers the most disturbing part of the contest. They begin at nine o'clock, an hour when I am never at my best, and the sight of other candidates *en masse* is most depressing. They all look so intelligent. They wear spectacles and use heavy fountain-pens whose barrels reflect their own mental capacity; once inside they write steadily and sternly, as though they were preparing leaders for the next week's *Lancet*; and the women students present such an aspect of concentration and industry it seems useless for men to continue the examination at all.

I went with a hundred other students into one of three large, square halls used for the examination. The polished wooden floor was covered with rows of desks set at a distance apart that made one's neighbour's writing completely indecipherable if he had not, as was usually the case, already done so himself. Each desk was furnished with a card stamped with a black examination number, a clean square of pink blotting-paper, and a pen apparently bought second-hand from the Post Office. The place smelt of floor-polish and freshly-sharpened pencils.

A single invigilator sat in his gown and hood on a raised platform to keep an eye open for flagrant cheating. He was helped by two or three uniformed porters who stood by the doors and looked impassionately down at the poor victims, like the policemen that flank the dock at the Old Bailey. The students scraped into their chairs, shot a hostile glance at the clock, and turned apprehensively to the buff question paper already laid out on each desk.

The first paper was on general medicine. The upper half of the sheet was taken up with instructions in bold print telling the candidate to write on one side of the paper only, answer all the questions, and to refrain from cribbing at peril of being thrown out. I brought my eyes painfully to the four questions beneath. At a glance I saw they were all short and pungent.

Give an account of the sign, symptoms, and treatment of heart failure was the first. 'Hell of a lot in that!' I thought. I read the second and cursed. *Discuss the changes in the treatment of pneumonia since 1930.* I felt the examiners had played a dirty trick by asking the same disease two papers in succession. The next simply demanded *How would you investigate an outbreak of typhoid fever?* and the last was a request for an essay on worms which I felt I could bluff my way through.

Three hours were allowed for the paper. About halfway through the anonymous examinees began to differentiate themselves. Some of them strode up for an extra answer book, with an awkward expression of self-consciousness and superiority in their faces. Others rose to their feet, handed in their papers, and left. Whether these people were so brilliant they were able to complete the examination in an hour and a half or whether this was the time required for them to set down unhurriedly their entire knowledge of medicine was never apparent from the nonchalant air with which they left the room. The invigilator tapped his bell half an hour before time; the last question was rushed through, then the porters began tearing papers away from gentlemen dissatisfied with the period allowed for them to express themselves and hoping by an incomplete sentence to give the examiners the impression of frustrated brilliance.

I walked down the stairs feeling as if I had just finished an eight-round fight. I reached desperately for my packet of cigarettes. The other candidates jostled round, chattering like children just out of school. In the square outside the first person I recognized was Grimsdyke.

'How did you get on?' I asked.

'So-so,' he replied. 'However, I am not worried. They never read the papers, anyway. I'm perfectly certain of that. Haven't you heard how they mark the tripos at Cambridge, my dear old boy? The night before the results come out the old don totters back from hall and chucks the lot down his staircase. The ones that stick on the top flight are given firsts, most of them end up on the landing and get seconds, thirds go to the lower flight, and any reaching the ground floor are failed. This system has been working admirably for years without arousing any comment. I heard all about it from a senior wrangler.'

Benskin's broad figure appeared among the crowd in the doorway. He was grinning widely and waved cheerily at us.

'You look pretty pleased with yourself,' I said.

'I am, old boy. To-day I tried out Benskin's infallible system for passing exams, and it worked beautifully. What number are you?'

'Three hundred and six.'

'I'm a hundred and ten. All I had to do was walk into the room labelled "Two to Three Hundred," wander round a bit while people got settled, and tell the invigilator chap they hadn't given me a place. He apologized at first, then he looked at my card and turfed me out pretty sharply to find the right room. I was pretty humble, of course, and murmured a lot of stuff about my nerves—however, in my wandering round the desks I'd taken damn good care to read all the questions. Now, if you look up the regulations you'll see candidates are admitted up to twenty minutes after the start of the examination, so I had plenty of time to dodge down to the lavatory and look it all up before presenting myself, breathless and distraught, at the correct room. Pretty smart, eh?'

'I hope they can't read your writing,' I said bitterly.

* * * * *

The oral examination was held a week after the papers. I got a white card, like an invitation to a cocktail party, requesting my presence at the examination building by eleven-thirty. I got up late, shaved with a new blade, and carefully brushed my suit. Should I wear a hospital tie? It was a tricky point. Examiners were well known for harbouring an allergy towards certain hospitals, and although my neckwear might convince them I was not from St. Mary's, for instance, or Guy's, my interrogators were quite as likely to be opposed to men from St. Swithin's.

I put on a quiet nondescript tie and a white stiff collar. The dressing-up was important, for the candidate was expected to look like a doctor even if he gave no indication of ever becoming one; one fellow who had once unhappily appeared in his usual outfit of sports coat and flannels was turned over to a porter by the outraged examiner with instructions to 'Show this gentleman to the nearest golf-course.'

It is the physical contact with the examiners that makes oral examinations so unpopular with the students. The written answers have a certain remoteness about them, and mistakes and omissions, like those of life, can be made without the threat of immediate punishment. But the viva is judgment day. A false

answer, an inadequate account of oneself, and the god's
brow threatens like an imminent thunderstorm. If the
candidate loses his nerve in front of this terrible displeasure he is finished: confusion breeds confusion
and he will come to the end of his interrogation
struggling like a cow in a bog. This sort of mental
attitude had already led to the disgrace of Harris, who
had been reduced to a state just short of speechlessness
by a terrible succession of *faux pas*. The examiner finally
decided to try the poor fellow with something simple
and handed him a breast-bone that had been partly
worn away with the life-long pressure of an enlarged
artery underneath. 'Now, my boy,' said the examiner.
'What do you think caused that hollow?' All he wanted
for a reply was the single word 'Pressure,' but Harris
looked at the specimen in blank silence. With a sigh,
the kindly examiner removed his pince-nez and indicated the two indentations they left on each side of his
nose. 'Well,' he continued helpfully, 'what do you think
caused that?' Something clicked in Harris's panicky
brain. The depressed nasal bridge . . . a picture flashed
up that he had seen so often in the opening pages of his
surgery book. 'Congenital syphilis, sir,' he replied
without hesitation.

I was shown to a tiny waiting-room furnished with
hard chairs, a wooden table, and windows that wouldn't
open, like the condemned cell. There were six candidates from other hospitals waiting to go in with me, all
of them in their best clothes. They illustrated the types
fairly commonly seen in viva waiting-rooms. There was
the Nonchalant, lolling back on the rear legs of his chair
with his feet on the table, showing the bright yellow
socks under his blue trouser-legs. He was reading the
sporting page of the *Express* with undeceptive thorough-

ness. Next to him, a man of the Frankly Worried class sat on the edge of his chair tearing little bits off his invitation card and jumping irritatingly every time the door opened. There was the Crammer, fondling the pages of his battered text-book in a desperate farewell embrace, and his opposite, the Old Stager, who treated the whole thing with the familiarity of a photographer at a wedding. He had obviously failed the examination so often he looked upon the viva simply as another engagement to be fitted into his day. He stood looking out of the window and yawning, only cheering up when he saw the porter, with whom he was now on the same warm terms as an undergraduate and his college servant.

'How are you getting on this time, sir?' the porter asked him cheerily.

'Not so dusty, William, not so dusty at all. The second question in the paper was the same one they asked four years ago. What are they like in there?'

'Pretty mild, this morning, sir. I'm just taking them their coffee.'

'Excellent! Put plenty of sugar in it. A low blood-sugar is conducive to bad temper.'

'I will, sir. Best of luck.'

'Thank you, William.'

The other occupant of the room was a woman. A trim little piece, I noticed, probably from the Royal Free. She sat pertly on her chair with her hands folded on her lap. Women students—the attractive ones, not those who are feminine only through inescapable anatomical arrangements—are under a disadvantage in oral examinations. The male examiners are so afraid of being prejudiced favourably by their sex they usually adopt towards them an undeserved sternness. But this girl had given care to her preparations for the examination. Her suit was neat but not smart; her hair tidy but not striking; she wore enough make-up to look attractive, and she was obviously practising, with some effort, a look of admiring submission to the male sex. I felt sure she would get through.

I sat alone in the corner and fingered my tie. They always made the candidates arrive too early, and the coffee would delay them further. There was nothing to do except wait patiently and think about something well removed from the unpleasant quarter of an hour ahead, such as rugby or the lady student's legs. Suddenly the door was flung open and a wild-eyed youth strode in.

'It's not too bad!' he exclaimed breathlessly to the nonchalant fellow. The two apparently came from the same hospital.

'I had Sir Rollo Doggert and Stanley Smith,' he said with a touch of pride. This brought a nod of appreciation from all of us, as they were known as two of the toughest examiners in London.

'Doggert started off by asking me the signs and symptoms of pink disease,' he continued. 'Luckily I knew that as I had happened to look it up last night . . .'

'Pink disease!' cried the worried man. 'My God, I forgot about that!'

'So I saw at once the way to handle him was to talk man-to-man, you know—none of this servile business, he much prefers to be stood up to. I reeled off pink disease and he said very good, my lad, very good.'

'Did he ask you anything else?' his friend said anxiously.

'Oh yes. He said, supposing I was out golfing with a diabetic who collapsed at the third tee, what would I do? Well, I said . . .'

The visitor gave a description of his examination in detail, like the man who comes out of the dentist's surgery and insists on telling the occupants of the waiting-room his experiences on the excuse that none of the frightful things that can happen really hurt.

The raconteur was stopped short by the porter. He marshalled us into line outside the heavy door of the examination room. There was a faint ting of a bell inside. The door opened and he admitted us one at a time, directing each to a different table.

16

'Y ou go to table four,' the porter told me.

The room was the one we had written the papers in, but it was now empty except for a double row of baize-covered tables separated by screens. At each of these sat two examiners and a student who carried on a low earnest conversation with them, like a confessional.

I stood before table four. I didn't recognize the examiners. One was a burly, elderly man like a retired prize-fighter who smoked a pipe and was writing busily with a pencil in a notebook; the other was invisible, as he was occupied in reading the morning's *Times*.

'Good morning, sir,' I said.

Neither of them took any notice. After a minute the burly fellow looked up from his writing and silently indicated the chair in front of him. I sat down. He growled.

'I beg your pardon, sir?' I said politely.

'I said you're number 306?' he said testily. 'That's correct, I suppose?'

'Yes, sir.'

'Well, why didn't you say so? How would you treat a case of tetanus?'

My heart leapt hopefully. This was something I knew, as there had recently been a case in St. Swithin's.

I started off confidently, reeling out the lines of treatment and feeling much better.

The examiner suddenly cut me short.

'All right, all right,' he said impatiently, 'you seem to know that. A girl of twenty comes to you complaining of gaining weight. What do you do?'

This was the sort of question I disliked. There were so many things one could do my thoughts jostled into each other like a rugger scrum and became confused and unidentifiable.

'I—I would ask if she was pregnant,' I said.

'Good God, man! Do you go about asking all the girls you know if they're pregnant? What hospital d'you come from?'

'St. Swithin's, sir,' I said, as though admitting an illegitimate parentage.

'I should have thought so! Now try again.'

I rallied my thoughts and stumbled through the answer. The examiner sat looking past me at the opposite wall, acknowledging my presence only by grunting at intervals.

The bell rang and I moved into the adjoining chair, facing *The Times*. The newspaper rustled and was set down, revealing a mild, youngish-looking man in large spectacles with a perpetual look of faint surprise on his face. He looked at me as if he was surprised to see me there, and every answer I made was received with the same expression. I found this most disheartening.

The examiner pushed across the green baize a small sealed glass pot from a pathology museum, in which a piece of meat like the remains of a Sunday joint floated in spirit.

'What's that?' he asked.

I picked up the bottle and examined it carefully. By

now I knew the technique for pathological specimens of this kind. The first thing to do was turn them upside down, as their identity was often to be found on a label on the bottom. If one was still flummoxed one might sneeze or let it drop from nervous fingers to smash on the floor.

I upturned it and was disappointed to find the label had prudently been removed. Unfortunately there was so much sediment in the jar that it behaved like one of those little globes containing an Eiffel Tower that on reversal cover the model with a thick snowstorm. I could therefore not even see the specimen when I turned it back again.

'Liver,' I tried.

'What!' exclaimed the surprised man. The other examiner, who had returned to his writing, slammed down his pencil in disgust and glared at me.

'I mean lung,' I corrected.

'That's better. What's wrong with it?'

I could get no help from the specimen, which was still tossing in swirling white particles, so I took another guess.

'Pneumonia. Stage of white hepatization.'

The surprised man nodded. 'How do you test diphtheria serum?' he demanded.

'You inject it into a guinea-pig, sir.'

'Yes, but you've got to have an animal of a standard weight, haven't you?'

'Oh yes . . . a hundred kilogrammes.'

The two men collapsed into roars of laughter.

'It would be as big as a policeman, you fool!' shouted the first examiner.

'Oh, I'm so sorry,' I stammered miserably. 'I mean a hundred milligrammes.'

The laughter was renewed. One or two of the examiners at nearby tables looked up with interest. The other candidates felt like prisoners in the condemned block when they hear the bolt go in the execution shed.

'You could hardly see it then, boy,' said the surprised man, wiping his eyes. 'The creature weighs a hundred grammes. However, we will leave the subject. How would you treat a case of simple sore throat?'

'I would give a course of sulphonamide, sir.'

'Yes, that's right.'

'I disagree with you, Charles,' the other interrupted forcibly. 'It's like taking a hammer at a nut. I have an excellent gargle I have been prescribing for years which does very well.'

'Oh, I don't know,' said the surprised fellow warmly. 'One must make use of these drugs. I've always had excellent results with sulphonamides.'

'Did you read that paper by McHugh in the *Clinical Record* last winter?' demanded the first examiner, banging the table again.

'Certainly I read it, George. And the correspondence which followed. Nevertheless, I feel it is still open to doubt——'

'I really cannot agree with you——'

They continued arguing briskly, and were still doing so when a second tinkle of the bell allowed me to slide out and rush miserably into the street.

* * * * *

The days after the viva were black ones. It was like having a severe accident. For the first few hours I was numbed, unable to realize what had hit me. Then I began to wonder if I would ever make a recovery and win through. One or two of my friends heartened me by describing equally depressing experiences that had overtaken them previously and still allowed them to pass. I began to hope. Little shreds of success collected together and weaved themselves into a triumphal garland. After all, I thought, I got the bottle right, and I knew about tetanus . . . then I forgot about it in my anxiety over the last section of the examination, the clinical.

The clinical is probably the most chancy of the three parts. The student may be allotted a straightforward case with sounds in the chest that come through his stethoscope like the noise of an iron foundry; or he may get something devilish tricky.

The cases for clinical examinations were collected from the out-patient departments of hospitals all over London, and were in the class referred to by physicians informally as 'old chronics.' They have their lesions healed as far as possible; now they walked round in fairly good health but with a collection of clicks, whistles, or rumbles inside them set up by the irreversible process of their diseases. These are just the sort of things examiners like presenting to students. A case of vague ill-health or an indefinite lump are too arguable, but a good hearty slapping in the chest gives a right to fail a man forthrightly if he misses it.

For this service the patients were given seven-and-six and free tea and buns. But most of them would happily have performed with a strictly amateur status and provided their own sandwiches. The six-monthly visits to the examination were their principal outings of the year. They attended their own hospitals monthly to show off the signs they proudly possessed to a single doctor and discuss their ailment with fellow-patients on the benches outside, but in the exam they were inspected by hundreds of doctors—or as good as—and chatted to the élite of fellow sufferers. It is .much the same as winning an international rugby cap.

I arrived at the examination building in plenty of time, to find out what I could of the cases from men who had already been examined. I knew Benskin had been in early and looked for him in the hall to ask what there was upstairs.

'There's an asthma in a red scarf, old boy,' he said helpfully. 'And an old man with emphysema just behind the door as you go in—if you get him be sure to examine his abdomen, he's got a couple of hernias thrown in.'

I made a mental note of it.

'Then there's a little girl with a patent ductus—you can't miss her, she's the only child in the room. Oh, and a woman with burnt-out tabes. He'll ask you what treatment you'd give her, and he expects the answer "None".'

I nodded, thanked him, and made my way to the examination room.

My first impression of the clinical examination was of a doctor's surgery gone into mass-production. Patients were scattered across the room on couches, beds, and wheel-chairs, the men divided from the women by screens across the centre. They were in all stages of undress and examination. Circulating busily between them were a dozen or so nurses, examiners in white coats, and unhappy students dangling their stethoscopes behind them like the tails of whipped puppies.

I was directed to a pleasant, tubby little examiner.

'Hello, my lad,' he began genially. 'Where are you from? Swithin's, eh? When are you chaps going to win the rugger cup? Go and amuse yourself with that nice young lady in the corner and I'll be back in twenty minutes.'

She was indeed a nice young lady. A redhead with a figure out of *Esquire*.

'Good morning,' I said with a professional smile.

'Good morning,' she returned brightly.

'Would you mind telling me your name?' I asked politely.

'Certainly. Molly Ditton, I'm unmarried, aged twenty-two, and my work is shorthand-typing, which I have been doing for four years. I live in Ilford and have never been abroad.'

My heart glowed: she knew the form.

'How long have you been coming up here?' I asked. 'You seem to know all the answers.'

She laughed.

'Oh, years and years. I bet I know more about myself than you do.'

Just the thing! There is a golden rule for clinical examinations—ask the patient. They attend the examination for so many years and hear themselves discussed so often with the candidates they have the medical terms off pat. All I had to do was play my cards correctly. I talked to her about Ilford, and the wonderful advantages of living there; of shorthand-typing and its effects on the fingernails; of her boy friends and her prospects of matrimony (this produced a few giggles); of the weather and where she went for her holidays.

'By the way,' I said with careful casualness, 'what's wrong with you?'

'Oh, I've mitral stenosis due to rheumatic fever, but I'm perfectly well compensated and I've a favourable prognosis. There's a presystolic murmur at the apex, but the aortic area is clear and there are no creps at the bases. By the way, my thyroid is slightly enlarged, they like you to notice that. I'm not fibrillating and I'm having no treatment.'

'Thank you very much,' I said.

The tubby man was delighted when I passed on to him the patient's accurate diagnosis as my own.

'Capital, capital!' he beamed. 'Spotted the thyroid, too . . . glad some of you young fellers use your powers of observation. Been telling my own students for years—observe, observe, observe. They never do, though. Right you are, my lad. Now just take this ophthalmoscope and tell me what you can see in that old woman's eye.'

My heart, which had been soaring like a swallow, took a sharp dive to earth. The examiner handed me the little black instrument with lenses for looking into the eye. I had often seen it used in the wards but I never seemed to find time to learn how to employ it myself. There was a knack to it, which I did not possess; and I knew plainly enough that the defect was sufficient to fail me out of hand. I imagined the examiner's sunny friendliness turning into a storm of irritation; my hand shook as I took the instrument. Slowly I placed it closely between my eye and the patient. All I could see was something that looked like a dirty tank in an aquarium with a large, dim fish in it. The time had come for quick thinking. Looking intently through the instrument I let out a long whistle of amazement.

'Yes, it is a big retinal detachment, isn't it?' the examiner said happily, taking away the ophthalmoscope and patting me on the back. I saw myself marked over the pass number, and with a grateful smile at the redhead tripped downstairs in elation.

In the hall I met Benskin again. He was looking profoundly miserable. 'What's up?' I asked anxiously.

Benskin shook his head and explained in a choked voice what had happened. While I was examining medical cases he had been questioned in practical midwifery. One of the tests for prospective obstetricians was provided by a life-size papier mâché model of half the female trunk, into which a straw-stuffed baby was slipped through a trapdoor. The candidate was then provided with a pair of obstetrical forceps and required to deliver it *per via naturalis*. This was demanded of Benskin. He solemnly applied the two blades to the head, taking care to put the correct one on first. He locked the handle, took it in the approved grip, and gave a strong pull. Nothing happened. He pulled harder, but the straw fœtus refused to be born. He felt sweat on his brow and his mouth went dry; he saw his chances of passing fading like a spent match. He gave a desperate heave. His feet slipped on the polished floor and over his head flew mother, baby, forceps and all.

The examiner looked at him lying on the floor for a second in silence. Then he picked up one blade of the forceps and handed it to him.

'Now hit the father with that,' he said sourly, 'and you'll have killed the whole bloody family.'

17

'ONE doesn't fail exams,' said Grimsdyke firmly. 'One comes down, one muffs, one is ploughed, plucked, or pipped. These infer a misfortune that is not one's own fault. To speak of failing is bad taste. It's the same idea as talking about passing away and going above instead of plain dying.'

We were sitting with Benskin in the King George. It was immediately after opening time in the morning and we were alone in the bar. We sat on stools, resting our elbows on the counter and our heads on our hands. All three of us looked pitifully dejected. The examination results were to be published at noon.

'It's the heartless way they do it,' I said. 'Picking you out one at a time in front of everybody. I wish they'd show a little decent discretion about the business. I'd much prefer it if they sent you a letter. You can at least slink away and open it in the lavatory or somewhere.'

'In Tibet, I believe,' Grimsdyke went on, 'they simply execute the unsuccessful candidates on the spot.'

'Well, they probably welcome it.'

'They failed Harris pretty decently,' Benskin said reverently, as though speaking of the dead. 'He's so sure he'll have to take it again in six months he's not even bothering to hear the results. When he floundered badly in his viva the old boy simply looked dreamily out of the window and said, "Young man, how mysterious and wonderful is Nature! Now we see the leaf turning gold on the branch and falling to the ground. The flowers and plants have lost their summer beauty and withered, and the earth looks dead beyond hope of resurrection. But in the month of April the spring will come, the trees will burst into green flames, the shoots will leap up through the black soil, and petals will cover the bare flowerbeds. And you and I, my boy, will be here to see it, won't we?" '

'I think that was very bad form,' said Grimsdyke.

The Padre put three small glasses in front of us.

'Whisky?' Grimsdyke said. 'I thought we ordered beer.'

'If you will permit me, Mr. Grimsdyke, I would like to suggest, on the basis of my experience, something a little more nourishing. I know what a difficult time this is for you young gentlemen. Will you please accept these with the compliments of the house?'

'Here, I say, Padre . . . !'

He held up his hand.

'Not a bit of it, sir. The money I have been obliged to take off you in our long acquaintance more than justifies it. Here's jolly good luck, gentlemen!'

'Bottoms up,' said Benskin.

'I'm sure I've failed, all the same,' I said, putting my glass down. 'How could I get through after that terrible viva?'

Benskin snorted.

'It's all very well for you to talk. What about my midwifery clinical? That came under the heading of ugly incidents.'

'You never know, my dear old boy,' Grimsdyke said

hopefully. 'You may have done brilliantly in the papers.'

'Let's not talk about it,' I said. 'Let's discuss rugger instead.'

*   *   *   *   *

At noon we arrived in the examination building. The same number of candidates were there, but they were a subdued, muttering crowd, like the supporters of a home team who had just been beaten in a cup tie.

We pushed our way into the large hall on the ground floor. It was packed full with anxious students. On the side of the hall facing us was the foot of a marble staircase. To the left of the staircase was a plain, open door, over which had been recently pinned a large black and white card saying 'EXIT.' To the right was a clock, which stood at a few minutes before twelve.

We had heard exactly what would happen. At midday precisely the Secretary of the Committee would descend the stairs and take his place, flanked by two uniformed porters, on the lowermost step. Under his arm would be a thick, leather-covered book containing the results. One of the porters would carry a list of the candidates' numbers and call them out, one after the other. The candidate would step up closely to the Secretary, who would say simply 'Pass' or 'Failed.' Successful men would go upstairs to receive the congratulations and handshakes of the examiners and failures would slink miserably out of the exit to seek the opiate of oblivion.

'One thing, it's quick,' Benskin muttered nervously.

'Like the drop,' said Grimsdyke.

One minute to twelve. The room had suddenly come to a frightening, unexpected silence and stillness, like an unexploded bomb. A clock tinged twelve in the distance. My palms were as wet as sponges. Someone coughed, and I expected the windows to rattle. With slow scraping feet that could be heard before they appeared the Secretary and porters came solemnly down the stairs.

They took up their positions; the leather book was opened. The elder porter raised his voice.

'Number two hundred and nine,' he began. 'Number thirty-seven. Number one hundred and fifty.'

The tension in the room broke as the students shuffled to the front and lined up before the staircase. The numbers were not called in order, and the candidates strained to hear their own over the low rumble of conversation and scraping of feet that rose from the assembly.

'Number one hundred and sixty-one,' continued the porter. 'Number three hundred and two. Number three hundred and six.'

Grimsdyke punched me hard in the ribs.

'Go on,' he hissed. 'It's you!'

I jumped and struggled my way to the front of the restless crowd. My pulse shot high in my ears. My face was burning hot and I felt my stomach had been suddenly plucked from my body.

I lined up in the short queue by the stairs. My mind was empty and numb. I stared at the red neck of the man in front of me, with its rim of blue collar above his coat, and studied it with foolish intensity. Suddenly I found myself on top of the Secretary.

'Number three oh six?' the Secretary whispered, without looking up from the book. 'R. Gordon?'

'Yes,' I croaked.

The world stood still. The traffic stopped, the plants

184

ceased growing, men were paralysed, the clouds hung in the air, the winds dropped, the tides disappeared, the sun halted in the sky.

'Pass,' the man muttered.

Blindly, like a man just hit by blackjack, I stumbled upstairs.

*   *   *   *   *

The bar of the King George was full. I crashed through the door like a hot wind.

'I've passed!' I screamed.

The bar rose in turmoil. I couldn't see any of it. It was a pink jumble of faces, a numb sensation of handshakes, a dim perception of backslapping.

'Congratulations, sir!' shouted the Padre, thrusting his hand through the mob. 'Congratulations, Doctor! Here you are, sir. A quart tankard, sir. With my every best wish.'

Someone pushed the deep pewter mug into my hands.

'Down the hatch!'

'One gulp, old man!'

I was too breathless to drink. I wanted to laugh, cry, dance, and run all at the same time.

'I can't believe it!' I exclaimed. 'It isn't true! The first thing I knew I was shaking hands with the old boys and signing my diploma.'

'How about the other two gentlemen?' the Padre called.

'Oh Lord!' I felt suddenly guilty. 'I'd quite forgotten to wait for them!'

At that moment the door flew open. There entered Benskin and Grimsdyke wearing each other's jackets, attempting to pull in with them a violently neighing carthorse.

'I think it's all right,' the Padre said.

The party went on until closing time. Every student in the school seemed to be inside the tiny bar. I emptied and re-emptied my tankard. Everyone was shouting and singing, leaning on each other, jostling their neighbours, slapping their friends on the back. The angry owner of the horse had been asked inside and was now singing The Lily of Laguna to a co-operative audience. The room filled tighter as the news of more successes was brought in, like victories to a triumphant headquarters.

'Bottle's through,' I heard Evans bawling over the hubbub. 'So's Sprogget.'

'How about you?' I shouted back.

Evans delightedly stuck his thumb in the air.

I suddenly found myself jammed between Benskin and Grimsdyke.

'Hooray!' shouted Benskin, ruffling my hair.

'It's bloody funny!' Grimsdyke shouted. 'Bloody funny!'

'What is?' I bawled at him.

'We're three bloody doctors,' he hollered.

We burst into roars of laughter.

*   *   *   *   *

My feelings in the next few days were those of a private unexpectedly promoted to general overnight. In a minute or two I had been transformed from an un-earning and potentially dishonest ragamuffin to a respectable and solvent member of a learned profession. Now banks would trust me with their money, hire firms with their cars, and mothers with their daughters. I could sign prescriptions, death certificates, and orders for extra milk, and no one could contradict me. It was wonderful.

As soon as the exam results were out the Chiefs made appointments to the resident staff of St. Swithin's. I became house-physician to Dr. Malcolm Maxworth, and had to begin work the next week. I saw from the list that Evans had been awarded the plum position of house-surgeon to the Professor, and Grimsdyke became a junior obstetrical officer. Sprogget had not bothered to apply for a job at St. Swithin's and Benskin was not given one. The Dean had vetoed the appointment.

I packed up and left the Bayswater flat. The landlord had been wanting to get rid of us for some time and took the opportunity of taking possession himself. We had a row about damages, but Sprogget settled it by threatening officially to report the plumbing to the local Medical Officer of Health unless the estimate was reduced considerably.

In the hospital I was given a small, bleak room with an iron bedstead, a desk, a chair, and a telephone. But I unpacked with delight—I was living there free of charge, and at last, at the age of twenty-three, I was earning some money.

There was a letter waiting for me, addressed ostentatiously to Dr. Gordon in Benskin's handwriting. I opened it.

'Dear old boy,' it began. 'I expect you will be surprised to hear that I have got married. As a matter of fact, I have for a long time been bloody keen on Molly (the nurse I proposed to that night), and we decided to do the old ring stuff as soon as I got through. I didn't say anything to you coarse fellows, because you have such warped ideas on such things. I have a job waiting for me in general practice at home, and we are now having the old honeymoon in Cornwall. Let me warn you against the swank of calling yourself doctor, old lad. I signed myself in the visitors' book as Dr. Benskin, and we had only just got into bed when the porter came banging on the door shouting at me that the cook had scalded herself. The marriage was consummated, but only just. Your old chum, Tony.'

'I'm damned!' I said. 'The old stoat!'

I was still staring at the letter when the 'phone rang. It was Sister Virtue, whom I now had to work with as a colleague. Her tone was only a little less severe than the one she used on students—to her, new housemen were hardly less reprehensible.

'Dr. Gordon,' she rasped. 'When are you going to appear in the ward? I have a stack of notes for you to sign and three new patients have been admitted. You can't expect the nursing staff to run the hospital on their own.'

I looked at my watch. It was six in the evening. I had to tell the Padre about Benskin.

'Half-past six, Sister,' I said. 'I've only just arrived. Will that be all right?'

'Not a minute later,' she snapped, discontinuing the conversation.

I walked across to the King George with Benskin's letter.

'I knew it all along, sir, if I may say so,' the Padre said calmly. 'It's always the same with the ones that run a mile if they see a nurse and talk big about staying single. I've seen it a good many times, now, sir. And you watch out, Dr. Gordon—I bet you're next.'

'Well, I don't know about that, Padre. There's no one on the cards at the moment.'

'Ah yes, sir, but wait till you've been about the

188

hospital a bit as a doctor instead of a student. Why, the nurses are all over you. You get proper spoilt, you lads do.'

'I must confess noting a certain sweet co-operation among the girls I hadn't found before. Perhaps you're right. Anyway, I'll watch my step.'

I took a few sips of my beer.

'It's quiet in here, Padre, to-night.'

'Early in the evening yet, sir.'

'I know . . . but it seems oppressively quiet, if you know what I mean. I suppose it's because there's been so much fun and games going on the last few days. It's . . . well, lonely. This qualification business is all very well, but it soon wears off. For about three days the world is at your feet, then you realize it's the beginning, not the end. You've got to fight a damn sight harder than you did in your exams to do your job decently and make a living.'

'That's right, sir. They all say the same. You've got to face it, them carefree student days is over for good. Life is hard, sir. It's bad enough for a publican, but a damn sight worse for a doctor.'

'Well, let's not get miserable about it,' I said. 'Still, these last few days I've begun to wish I'd got a bit more out of my education.'

'Come off it, sir,' said the Padre genially. 'You've made a lot of friends, which mark my words you'll hang on to till your dying day. And that's valuable, sir. A lot of people can get an education, but not many of 'em can collect as sound a bunch of good friends as you young gentlemen do. Wherever you go, sir, no matter how many years to come, you'll still remember Mr. Benskin and the rest and the good times you've had in these four walls.'

'You know, Padre,' I said, 'that's exactly what I think myself. I was just too frightened to say so.'

The door opened. A porter stood there.

'Dr. Gordon,' he said. 'I've been looking for you all over. Wanted at once in the ward, sir. Emergency just come in.'

I looked at the half-full glass of beer. I picked it up. hesitated, and left it.

'All right,' I said, pulling my stethoscope out of my pocket. 'I'm coming.'

Times have changed, I thought as I walked over to the hospital. I suddenly realised that from now on it was always going to be like this.